PANDORA'S BOX

DEMON QUEEN SERIES, BOOK 2

EVE NEWTON

Dear Leah,

Lots of Love

Eve Newton

Demon Queen Series, Book 2

Copyright © Eve Newton, 2020

Exclusive to Amazon. If you purchase or download a copy from any other website, this is illegal pirating.

This book is a work of fiction. Any references to historical events, real people, or real locales are used fictitiously. Other names, characters, places, and incidents are products of the author's imagination, and any resemblance to actual events or locales or persons, living or dead, is entirely coincidental.

CHAPTER 1

Annabelle

I STAND on the frozen ground, completely stunned as I look out around the white landscape. I shiver and it's not only because of the cold.

"What did you do?" Killian asks as he strides towards me.

"What makes you think *I* had anything to do with this?" I reply, mock wounded.

"You are trouble, Princess," he says with a sigh and rubs his hand over his face.

"Well, not going to argue with that but this wasn't me."

"Can you fix it?" he asks earnestly.

I understand his concern. We have just put Hell under lockdown. Throwing a different climate at them with no prior warning and one where the majority of them don't even know what snow is, isn't the best thing to have happened today.

"Not sure," I murmur as I spot a Demon walking towards us.

She is a female, with light blonde hair and as she gets

closer, I see her ice-blue eyes linger on Killian for a minute before they land on me. She gives me a thorough appraisal that kind of makes me wish I was naked, instead of bundled up in fighting gear and my huge coat.

"Our Queen, right?" she asks me before she turns back to Killian. "Killian. Nice to see you again."

I narrow my eyes at her and step a little bit closer to *my* male, just in case she decides to get any ideas about jumping on him right in front of me.

"Xavi," Killian says with a brief nod in her direction. Then, he looks back at me blandly, which makes me want to giggle like an idiot.

He absolutely has no clue that this female would do him in a heartbeat if he gave the word.

She looks at me and holds her hand out. "Xavier, Your Majesty. Horseman of Pestilence."

I balk at her openly.

I never really thought about Pestilence as a gorgeous, blue-eyed, blonde female before. I'd kind of expected a skanky Demon with pustules and shit all over his face.

Just shows you how wrong you can be.

I reach out for her hand and grip it tightly, giving her a once-over that she cracks an icy smile at.

"Not what you expected?"

"Not at all," I admit.

"I get that a lot."

"I bet," I murmur.

She releases my hand. "I have returned from my assignment on Earth. I think you will be incredibly pleased with the outcome of the pandemic sweeping across the globe."

"Hm, I'm sure."

"I could tell you all about it over a drink," she says, stepping a bit closer.

I gaze into her astonishing eyes. "I can read the report

that you give to Roberta," I say, wondering what the Hell she is up to. She is now looking at me like she wants to eat out my pussy, and while I wouldn't say 'no', I'm not sure my males would appreciate it. Killian especially, as I hear him let out a low rumble when Xavier reaches out to pull my coat apart and dips her finger into my cleavage.

"Where is the fun in that?" she purrs.

"Hands off, Xavi," Killian growls at her, giving her a not-so-gentle shove backwards.

She raises her perfect eyebrow at him before understanding dawns. "I see," she murmurs, leaning in closer to me again. "Come and find me if you want that drink."

"I don't chase."

"Don't expect you have to. I'll be easy to find."

With that said, she disappears in an icy whirlwind of strong sulfur-smelling smoke, leaving me madly curious, a little bit sweaty and definitely turned on.

I give Killian a bright smile and loop my arm through his. "We need to gather the troops and sort out this mess."

He nods briskly and before I can flame us back to my bedroom, he sends us to another room down the hall with a bolt of lightning that I *swear* he made hit me on my ass in the process.

Asshole.

"What?" I snap at him, shaking my arm loose.

"I have never been a possessive male, Princess, but seeing you out there flirting with Xavi has brought out a primal instinct in me that I didn't think existed," he snarls.

I try not to laugh.

He seems so pissed off about it, poor Horseman.

I take off my coat now that we are back indoors and fold my arms. "Jealous?" I taunt him.

He grabs me by my shoulders, dragging me to him. "Yes," he spits out. "Happy?"

3

"Very," I murmur. "I feel the same about you." I drop my defensive stance and reach up to place my hand on the back of his neck. "I want to brand you with my initial like a fucking steer, so that everyone knows that you belong to me."

His eyes flash dangerously. "Try it and see what happens," he rasps darkly.

I can't resist a challenge. His whole attitude is turning me on badly now after already being lit up by Xavier.

I give him a triumphant smile as I bring the fires of Hell to the hand resting on his neck.

He grunts and drops to his knees as I exert more pressure on him.

"That's it, baby. Kneel for me. I own you and now everyone will know."

I pull my hand away and admire my handiwork. A nice big red 'A' has been burnt into his skin for all eternity.

"Bitch," he snarls at me and knocks me off my feet with one swipe of his huge arm.

"Fuck!" I roar as I hit the deck hard and then let out a whoosh of air as he lands on top of me, his face furious.

He fumbles with the zipper on my leather pants, which only riles me up further. I push my hips up, ready for some action, but he slams me back down, with both of his hands. He grabs the top of my pants and drags them down.

The spark in my blood is something that excites me, but at the same time, that teeny tiny pang of fear at the look on his face makes me fight against him.

"Hold still, Princess," he growls. "You want to brand me? See how you like it when I brand your pussy with *my* initial and your other lovers have to stick their dick in it knowing that I possess you."

"Fuck you!" I screech like a banshee. No way is he getting his fucking hands on me, treating me like his bitch.

I struggle underneath him, and I'm seriously impressed by his strength. He has been around since Hell began, as he said, he's inevitable. But he shouldn't be able to hold me for long.

With my pants down my thighs, I scream in his face and flame out to my bedroom, only to find to my utter disgust that not only am I still on the floor, but he came with me because he was touching me. What the actual fuck? I can flame out solo even if someone is hanging on to me for dear life.

"Asshole!" I snarl.

"Told you, darlin', you're strong but my power is as connected to this place as yours is. Now hold still!"

"Fuck! You!" I shout, squirming to get away from him.

"Annie?" Devlin asks, peering over the side of the bed with a serious case of bedhead affecting his usually careful spiked-up hair. "What? Get the fuck off her!" He climbs off the bed, completely naked, a semi bouncing in front of him.

"Oh no," Killian says with victory flashing in his eyes as he places his palm over my pussy.

I hiss, arching my back as his hand heats up and the smell of burning flesh hits my nose.

"Bastard," I growl as he smirks at me,

He removes his hand and I look down to see he has in fact burned a 'K' on my mound.

I smirk back. "That'll be gone in a second."

He raises his eyebrow at me and looks down.

I wait.

Devlin waits, mouth agape.

It doesn't heal.

"Are you fucking kidding me?" I rant as I get to my feet and drag my pants back up, high enough to walk over to the mirror. "How the fuck?" I stare at my perfect pussy in the mirror that is now branded.

5

"Tit for tat," Killian says, sneaking up behind me and placing his hands on my shoulders. "Now we belong to each other in a way that is irrefutable."

"How?" I ask again, baffled by how he has managed to hurt me.

He kisses the top of my head as the other males, now all fully awake and functional after our tussle, grimace at my reflection in the mirror.

I deftly zip up my pants and turn to face them.

"Glad you're all awake," I say, ignoring the branding on the pussy for now. "Shit has hit the fan. We need to talk. Meet me in the Dining Hall in ten minutes." I give Killian a scathing look. "I'm going to shower."

I stalk off to the en-suite before anyone has a chance to say anything, and slam the door behind me.

I snap my fingers and stand in front of the mirror naked. I shake my head and then shrug.

Well, I guess he did warn me about seeing what would happen if I branded him. Did he know that a mark from his hand would stay on my skin, though? That is the burning question, pardon the pun.

After he marked me back, he didn't seem all that pissed about it. If anything, he seemed pleased that we had done this to each other.

I sigh as I don't want to think too deeply about it. He is probably just glad to have been able to reinforce his position as the Alpha male around here. It probably doesn't have anything to do with his parting words to me, which if I think about too much, will only make me regret it.

"Damn you," I mutter, wishing that he wasn't a Demon and that I *could* actually damn him. "You are going to hurt me, aren't you?"

I turn from the mirror and step into the shower, turning

on the jets full blast and scorching hot. The bathroom steams up quickly, but I don't feel the heat on my skin.

Cold? Now that's a different story and if Shax had anything to do with this, I will kick his ass back down here so fast his head will spin. Then, I'll chain him up in the dungeon so that he can never leave again and fuck with my domain.

If he *didn't* have anything to do with it, then…I sigh again. "Where are you, bro? I fucking need you."

I place my head on the tiles for a brief moment and then draw in a deep breath. I straighten up, clean off. When I step out of the shower minutes later, I'm back to my old self and, picking up Babe, I stride forward, ready to fix this problem the only way I know how, by being a ruthless badass with the power of Hell on my side.

I mean…how hard can it be?

CHAPTER 2

Annabelle

I FLAME into the Dining Hall to see all of my males assembled around the huge table, including Gregory. He gives me a tentative smile, which I return with a confident beam. It immediately relaxes him. There is no doubt that being around these Demons without me must be unnerving for him. He is handling it well, although Devlin appears to be keeping an eye on him. As in, he is taking more than a passing interest in my human. I wonder if it delves past his Necromancer part onto a sexier level.

I tingle in all the right places at that thought.

I cast a glance over Killian, who has taken it upon himself to sit at the head of the table, and everyone else has joined him up there. I sneer at him. Who the fuck does he think he is?

I stalk down the twenty-seater to the other head and sit down. I slam Babe down on the table, calling this meeting to order. I wait while the males scramble to join me on the other side. Killian gives me a smirk to let me know that he did it on purpose to see what I would do.

I kick out the chair to my right and he takes it, sitting his massive frame down. Elijah sits on my left, Aleister next to him. Gregory is next to Aleister with Devlin opposite him, his feet on the table. Drescal, always having to be the one who outshines them all, stands next to me, his hand on the back of my chair. I smile up at him and he bends to kiss my forehead.

"Still there?" he murmurs.

"Yep," I say, then press my lips together as I look back at the males.

The flash of danger in his eyes was unmistakable.

I snap my fingers and Roberta appears, looking flustered and perplexed, her hair a mess all over her head and her light gray, elasticated-waist skirt askew from having burst through space and time against her will.

I give her an ingratiating smile. "Roberta. Have you seen the outside?"

"I have, Your Majesty," she clips out, recovering with speed. "With all due respect, Ma'am…what the fuck?"

I snort. "Indeed. I have no idea. Has anything like this happened before at all in the history of Hell?"

She shakes her head immediately.

"Wait!" Drescal interjects. "What's happened?"

"Go and see," I reply, waving my hand at them.

All the males that can transport themselves outside go, leaving me and Gregory looking at each other awkwardly, with Killian still seated as he already knows about our predicament.

Roberta stands there silently, for once showing a bit of respect. Maybe she has been stunned into supplication by the snow.

I snicker to myself, receiving odd looks from the three of them, but I shake my head.

The males return, covered in snow, expletives of all kinds filling the silence.

"Snow?" Devlin asks rhetorically, shaking it off his black duster.

I wait for them all to seat themselves again.

"Roberta?" I prompt.

"Nothing whatsoever," she says. "This is…new." She gives me an accusing look for a brief moment before she resumes a neutral expression.

"You sure?" I press, just in case.

"Very, Ma'am."

"Thanks," I mutter. "Please ensure that Darius and his army are prepared for every eventuality. This is going to throw the Demons and coupled with a lockdown, I don't want to be the one to go out there and sort out my minions if they get unruly."

She bobs her head, clearly in full agreement. The more Demons I kill off, the harder her job is.

I wave my hand and send her on her way.

"Snow?" Elijah growls.

I'm getting agitated by his troubled attitude. I stand up and start to pace.

I feel Gregory's eyes on me, so I stop and look at him.

"You feel that Shax leaving has something to do with this?" he asks quietly, stopping the further rumbling complaints from the males about being wet and cold.

I tap my foot. "Possibly," I say, after a hefty pause.

"Why do you think that?" Aleister asks quietly.

The rage fires up and I kick out at the chair I'd been sitting in, watching it skitter across the room.

"Because Hell was fine and then he left, and this happened!" I snap, feeling my wings pop out and flap wildly.

All of the males head for the hills, diving off theatrically to the sides, Devlin taking Gregory with him.

Everyone, that is, except Killian. He sits back and gives me a bland look.

I hiss as the Shift is ready to take me over. If I do that, I'm risking everyone in here.

"One, two, three and smile," Gregory calls out from underneath the table.

I take in a deep breath and mutter, "One, two, three and smile." I force a beam on my face, my hands clenched at my sides.

"Nicely done," Gregory's voice states proudly.

I throw Aleister an apologetic smile as he ventures closer now that I seem to have my temper under control. He knows my anger isn't at him, it's at my twin for abandoning me.

"Annabelle," he says in that calm way that he has.

"What?" I ask, as all the males come closer and peer at me in fascination. "What?" I growl when no one says anything.

"Your wings have grown bigger and a lot more intricate," Drescal says, moving in as close as he dares. "You are spectacular."

"Oh," I say and look over my shoulder at my wings. "Oh!" I say in wonder as I see what he means.

"Beautiful," Killian mutters. "I can't wait to fuck you that way."

"Mm," I murmur, wanting that as well.

But then I shake my head. We need to sort out this mess first.

"I think Shax is with the box," I say, stashing my wings and sitting back down in the chair that Elijah recovered for me from across the room. I give him a nod of thanks.

"I need to go and see the Hounds," he says, remaining standing and looming over me as he puts his hand on the table.

I purse my lips at him.

"They will be frantic with this change and they need feeding anyway. I've left them for too long," he insists.

"Don't linger. If Darius finds you…"

"You'll get me out of it," he replies with a gruff laugh. "Besides, I wouldn't go down without a fight and I'm itching for something to hit."

"That's…aggressive," I point out, to the amusement of the assembled males.

"Pot, kettle, Queenie. I'm going," he states, straightening up.

"What about *my* shit?"

"Lian will catch me up," he murmurs and bends down to kiss me gently on my lips.

I grimace at him, but how can I be angry with him for looking after his Hounds and prioritizing their needs? He totally should. They can't sort themselves out. I can.

"Take Mouse," I call after him as he gives me a wave.

He lets out a loud, ear-piercing whistle and she comes bounding out of the main hallway to join him.

"So back to the box and Shax. They are together? How do you know?" Drescal asks, taking Elijah's seat before anyone else can scoot over.

"Earlier, I was with Sid in a dream. I saw the box and all this mist. I knew Shax was there, but I couldn't see him. Sid confirmed it. He is weirdly connected to him as well now." I screw up my face as I still don't understand that connection. "Anyway, find Shax, find the box."

"Why do you think he's keeping it from you?" Aleister asks a damn good question.

"I'm not sure."

"Earth?" Devlin asks.

I shake my head. "I didn't get that feel."

"If you go up there...the consequences will be dire," Killian finally speaks up.

"I know," I say lightly, avoiding Gregory's eyes. I haven't told him the whole truth about me.

"If you need to go to find the box and Shax, then you need to go," Gregory says. "Aren't you a rule-breaker?" He gives me a smile.

"Usually," I say. "But this is different."

"Why?" he asks, cottoning on that I'm hiding something.

"You haven't told him?" Devlin asks, leaning forward. "Aren't we supposed to be all in, Annie?"

I frown at him. Why is he being so fucking protective over Gregory?

"Told me what?" Gregory asks carefully.

I sigh and run my hand through my hair. "My destiny is so much more than this," I state, gesturing around. "My father required me to be born for a very specific task."

"What's that then?" he inquires quietly.

"She's the fucking Anti-Christ!" Devlin exclaims, getting pissed off with all of this back and forth. "She walks the Earth, she starts Armageddon."

I scowl furiously at my Necromancer for being the biggest asshole in Hell. "Dev," I hiss at him. I purposely didn't tell Gregory about this because 'Demon Queen' is way easier to swing and put a spin on it that he could accept. If I'd thrown out the words 'Anti-Christ' at him, the resounding connotations of that would have been epic.

"Anti-Christ?" he repeats faintly.

"Yep," I say brashly. Might as well fucking own it now.

"Apocalypse?" he stammers, looking over at Killian and shrinking back slightly in his chair.

"That's right."

"Fuuuuck," he says and then slams his lips shut.

"So, you see that going there is not a decision to be taken

lightly. However, I'm not sure Earth is the right place to look."

"Is there any way to do a locator spell on it?" Drescal asks.

"No, I've tried. It's protected."

"But what if we all add our combined force to the spell?" Devlin asks, pulling a cigarette out of a pack and lighting it.

"Hmm…" I give Devlin a lingering look.

"Not just a pretty face," he snickers.

"But it's a big part, gorgeous," I tease.

He beams and draws on his cigarette. "Think about it. Who knows? At this point, it's worth taking a shot, yeah?"

"Yeah. Give me a while, okay. If we do have to go to Earth, I need to think about the best way to handle it."

They all agree, and I stand up.

"Oh, don't all be heroes and head outside. Darius *does not* mess about. Elijah has shit to do, the rest of you stay put."

Aleister raises his hand as if he's in class. "Uhm, I have to head back to the Rooftop. You know, also got shit to do." His smile is slow and sexy. I nearly swoon.

"Yeah, forgot about you," I giggle. "Go, but be safe."

"He can't catch me up there," he replies and points up. He stands and swoops in to give me a kiss on the lips and then he is gone.

"Well," I huff. "Anyone else I have to worry about?"

"Nope," Devlin says. "You're not getting rid of me now that I'm here."

"Good," I say. "I'll be in my room. I'll contact Sid, see if he can shed some light on where Shax is. I know his leaving is behind Hell freezing over. He needs to return, there's nothing else for it. Feel free to wander around the residence to wherever your heart desires."

After picking up Babe, I stalk off, my thoughts reeling. It all just makes perfect sense all of a sudden. Shax leaving has fucked with Hell and left *me* vulnerable. Killian was able to do what he did because of it.

I can't help the burst of laughter that escapes when I wonder if Shax has a matching 'K' imprinted in his dick area. Serves him fucking right if he does.

CHAPTER 3

Gregory

"Wait," I call after Annabelle.

She pauses in one of the small corridors that leads off the Dining Hall and turns around. She has the bat resting at her side and a smile on her face.

"You okay?" she asks.

I nod. "I'm fine. I just…" I swoop into her personal space and drag her towards me, pressing my lips to hers.

I kiss her softly at first, but when she opens up for me, I delve my tongue into her mouth tasting her. I hear her bat clunk to the floor as she leans into me, wrapping her arms around me and sliding her hand up to the back of my neck.

She sighs and pulls away a moment later, her eyes searching mine.

"I'm ready," I croak out, needing her to know that I'm not afraid of her and her newly revealed role as the Anti-Christ.

"No, you aren't. You're doing this to prove to yourself that you're okay with what you now know about me," she says, her eyes lowering as she kicks the bat at her feet gently.

"I am," I insist. "I want to be with you." I know that I do, I know what it entails.

She shakes her head, looking back up at me with those remarkable green eyes. "You have no idea how hard it is to say 'no' to you right now, Gregory, but I have to. I can't let you in unless I know you're one hundred percent committed to me and this life."

"I *am* committed to you," I say, anger getting the better of me. She is telling me how I feel, and it is pissing me off.

"Anti-Christ," she says and then presses her lips together.

Okay, I flinched. How could I not? She has the ability to end the world with two footsteps on the Earth's soil.

"See," she whispers and turns from me,

I grab her arm, not wanting her to go. "Annabelle, please, listen to me…"

A stinging pain shoots through my hand and up my arm. I stumble back to see Drescal leaning casually up against the wall behind us.

"The lady said, 'no'," he says.

I grimace at him as Annabelle tuts. "That's not fair, Dres. Don't use your powers on him."

If I'd thought I was angry before, that was an understatement. My temper zings up a notch as she defends me against having my arse kicked by Drescal's magick. So, she has a point. I wouldn't stand a chance against a nine-hundred-year-old Demon, but it still stings.

"I'm ready and I will prove it to you," I snap at her and turn on my heel to stalk off.

"Gregory, wait!" she calls after me, but I ignore her.

I don't want to discuss this further with Drescal hanging around and a part of me hopes she will come after me.

She doesn't.

It doesn't surprise me. There is no reason in Hell, why she would chase me.

I sigh and make my way back to my rooms on the ground floor. I pull up short as I realize that I'm living downstairs, while they are all residing *upstairs.*

I make a decision. One that I would never have contemplated making before I came here. I storm through my office and into my bedroom. I start to pack up the few belongings that Annabelle bestowed on me and the fewer things that Shax went back to Earth for, a few weeks after he abducted me. I stuff it all in the holdall that Shax handed me wordlessly such a short time ago but seems like forever. Not in an all bad way. I just feel that I have lived here longer than I have.

I march back out of my bedroom and back through the office, heading for the main staircase in the residence. Ascending them two at a time, I arrive at the top and look all the way down the long corridor to Annabelle's bedroom door.

Then I count a few doors down and walk over to the one that sits four down on the left. Judging by my count, I expect it to be unlived in.

I'm right. It is made up, nice and tidy, but belongs to no one.

Until now.

"Making yourself at home?" Devlin asks, appearing next to me in a swirl of black air.

"Why not? Everyone else is," I snap, still pissed off at Annabelle's rebuff.

"She'll be pleased," he replies, ignoring my shitty attitude.

"Sorry," I murmur, feeling the need to apologize for my mood.

"She wants you, but if you decide that Hell isn't for you...

you'll hurt her. She is, for once, thinking with her head and not her heart," Devlin informs me.

"Hell *is* for me," I retort. "She gave me an out and I stayed."

"I'll ask you again in a hundred years."

"I'll be dead by then."

Blue eyes sparkle. "Like I said, I'll ask you again."

I smirk at him, ignoring the spike of fear that races through my veins at his words, and putting on a front. "Sure thing."

"There are ways to prolong your existence," he starts, but I hold my hand up.

"Don't. We've already talked about that."

"I doubt you discussed *all* of the options," he says.

"And?" I ask shortly. "What is *your* suggestion for this?"

"Not for me to say. Just know that if you do end up growing old and dying, you will be leaving her, thus hurting her. You aren't all in unless you make a real choice, Doc." He vanishes the same way he arrived, leaving me indignant, but with a lot to think about. Does she really want me to become a Demon so that I'll be immortal? What kind of Demon? A Vampire? That seems the easiest choice. A quick bite and I'm done. I think. Unless the movies have it wrong. I'll still be me, but with fangs.

I gulp as I realize I will have to live on blood for the rest of eternity.

I sigh and sit heavily on the bed. Devlin is right. I have a *real* choice to make and I have to make it sooner rather than later.

CHAPTER 4

Shax

I STARE at the box in front of me and then I look at Shadow. She shrugs, leaving this whole situation to me. I don't blame her. What Vazna is asking of me is…it's unfathomable.

I sigh and look back at the box.

Then, with an annoyed huff, I turn around and stalk off to the side of the cloud and look down over the Earth.

I'm not in Heaven. More like a pit stop on the way to Heaven. I glare down at the blue and green ball and wish that I was standing on it with Shadow, doing what I set out to do, not standing on a fucking cloud miles up in the sky with Sophie's fucking Choice on my hands.

"Hey," Shadow says, coming up behind me. "What is your first instinct telling you to do?"

"Take the box to Annabelle," I reply without even thinking.

I breathe in and look down at her.

"Then do it."

"That simple?"

"Yes, it is, Shax. You hold all the power here. *Luc* gave you all the power. He knew you would do the right thing."

"And what if the right thing turns out to be the wrong thing?" I ask earnestly.

She giggles. "Never met a creature of Hell that worried about that," she says lightly.

"That's the problem though, isn't it? Am I a creature of Hell or not?"

"You've just proved that your loyalty lies with your sister. Ask yourself what that means," she says, standing up on her tiptoes to kiss me softly on the mouth.

I return it, flicking my tongue against her lips until she opens up. I kiss her deeply, finding solace in her embrace. It is the only thing that gives me this feeling but as much as I want to continue, I have to make a decision and soon. All of this pissing about is annoying me.

I pull back and regard her yellow eyes, searching for the answer in them. Is she right? Does my gut instinct prove that I belong in Hell with Annabelle or does it just prove that I will side with my sister, my *twin*? Further, does it only prove that I'm no one without her and that I need her to make a decision for me?

I growl, getting more and more pissed off as the seconds tick by.

Shadow stays silent, seeing that the struggle is real. Then she speaks, breaking the silence.

"If you do what Vazna wants you to do, you will be betraying your sister. If you *don't* do what he asks, then you will be setting free Lucifer to potentially demand his rule back from Annabelle and possibly hurt her in the process. I don't know much about relationships, but I do know that you love your sister more than anything. Both of these options might hurt her, but ask yourself which one will hurt her less?"

I glower at her.

"I don't know anything about Annabelle as your sister, but I do know our Queen. She will kick your ass from Hell to the Wastelands and back if you betray her."

I can't help snickering. It's true. She would.

I sigh.

"Vazna says that I am the only one who can open this box or destroy it with my blood. Inside is both Luc and Lucifer, along with Luc's father. Three generations of the Devil that are all still alive, in some respect, that will change the balance of the fucking *universe* if they are all set free."

"Luc wanted you to destroy it," Shadow points out gently. "But I know you can't do that to your sister. If you kill her father…"

"I know. But Luc knew. He knew I was the key to ending Lucifer once and for all, along with himself and his father. I know he has done this so that Annabelle's rule will never be really challenged or put into doubt. He wants me to destroy this box with all of them inside so that she is free to be who she was always meant to be."

"Do you trust that Vazna is telling the truth about Luc's wishes?" she ventures.

I nod and gesture to the letter that he'd handed me a while ago. It is written in Luc's handwriting with the word *Credo* at the bottom. It's that one word that makes me know this letter came from Luc. It was his last word to me before he was put into the painting. I thought he was telling me to trust in Annabelle but now I know it was so much more than that.

"Yes, it's Luc's letter. He knew that Vazna, that Heaven, would be on the same side of this. It's why he entrusted the box to him. If I destroy this box, I lose Hell; I take this box to Belle, I lose Heaven, or at least any chance that I had of exploring it."

"Why don't we fly for a while? Up here, no one will see us. Be free for a while, Shax. Do what you came here to do. It may give you clarity."

I smile. "Now that's a decision that I don't even have to think about," I say as I sprout my black-feathered wings.

Shadow grins at me and strips off her clothes. She Shifts in the next second and is swooping off the cloud in her magnificent Griffin form and I follow, leaving the weight of the decision that I must make when I get back on the cloud as we swoop through the sky – free.

CHAPTER 5

Annabelle

I HAVE BEEN STANDING outside Shax's bedroom door for an inordinate amount of time. Drescal tried to join me, but I wasn't in the mood after he used his power on Gregory. I told him to get lost and he did.

Poor Incubus. I will have to find him later and make it up to him.

I wish that I could trust Gregory's words, but I don't. I saw the flash of fear when I threw those two words at him. I *knew* it would happen, that's why I've never mentioned it to him before.

I move forward and shove the door to the bedroom open. I can smell Shax all around the room and it makes me want to cry.

"Asshole," I mutter. "What have you done to me?"

I close the door quietly and lean against it. It's dark, but I can still see the vial on the dresser with a note shoved underneath it.

I walk over and pick up the vial. I know instantly that it is

24

his blood. It is hot to my touch through the glass. I pick up the note.

Belle,

I knew you'd come in here, you nosy bitch. Don't look under the bed, it will shock you!
This vial should last you until I get back. Proof that I won't be gone long, sweet sister.
Keep calm & kick ass.
Love S.

I blink back my tears and put the vial in between my tits for safe keeping. I replace the note carefully on the dresser and then I drop to my knees and crawl over to the bed, lifting the covers up so that I can peer underneath.

I let out a snort of epic proportions as I pull the shallow box towards me and I see what's inside. "Really? You dark horse, you," I murmur, quite impressed with my brother's lack of inhibition in that area. "Who knew?"

I shove it back under the bed and then sit with my back leaning against it. After a moment, I climb onto the bed and drag the covers over me and curl up, covering myself. I press my hand between my legs and smile.

After the initial shock of what Killian did to me, it's kinda turning me on now. It's fucking sexy and I don't care about his motivations for doing it. My pussy belongs to him. Okay, yeah, he has to share, but there's no going back from what he did. I wonder if he hoped it wouldn't last and that it'd heal like it was supposed to.

I'm feeling all sorts of turned on now and slip my hand into my pants only to drag it back out when I remember where I am. Rubbing one out in your twin brother's room is icky, even for me.

I feel myself start to drift off. Sid had woken me way too early to tell me about Hell freezing over and it's been a trying few hours since then.

"Annabelle," Sid says, slipping his hand into mine.

I smile up at him. "Sid, where are you? Why aren't you with me?"

He looks away. "I feel safer where I am," he mutters after a long pause.

"From me?" I ask lightly.

He shrugs.

"I'm not going to hurt you, Sid. I want you with me."

"Why?" he asks shyly. "Why me?"

"Hey," I say, reaching up to turn his face towards mine. I get up on my tiptoes to kiss his lips. "I want you."

He sighs. "It's been a long time since someone said that to me. She hurt me."

I swallow. The opportunity is there, and I have to seize it or regret it. "Leviathan?" I ask gently.

He nods, keeping his eyes averted.

"What happened?"

"We were close once, but I grew to dislike her. We were quite different. I ended things with her. She grew angry and burned me with Hellfire." He shrugs.

"Oh, Sid," I murmur, stroking his scarred face. "I would never do that. I hope that you know that."

"Trust is...hard for me," he says. "I like to be safe. I was safe in prison. No one to hurt me."

"You feel it will be too much to come out of Razor and reclaim your life. I understand, Sid, but I want to be with you. I can't do this in my head all the time. It's not the same."

"I can't," he whispers. "Not with all of them."

"Them?" I ask with a frown.

"They are better than me. Even the Hellhound. He is scarred but he isn't like me."

"Oh, Sid. Don't ever think that you aren't good enough. I want to love you, but you have to give me a chance." I wrap my arms around him.

It takes a moment, but he returns my embrace tightly.

"Come to me," I murmur.

He nods and then vanishes. I stumble as I find myself hugging air instead of him.

"Annabelle."

I wake up and blink.

"Hi," I say with a smile.

"Hi," Sid says. He is lying next to me on the bed.

"Are you sticking around?" I ask, turning my body to face him.

"I'll try," he says, resigned. "For you. I will do anything for you."

"Good," I say with a beam and then lean forward to press my lips to his.

He jerks his head back, giving me a look of horror.

"What?" I ask, propping myself up on my elbow. "You don't want to kiss me?" I add quietly.

"I do, but…"

"Sid," I say sternly. "Stop this right now." I figure there is only one way to push past this. I grab his shirt and drag him towards me. I climb on top of him, pressing him into the bed. I give him a slow smile and then I lean down to kiss him again. I flick my tongue against his lips until he eventually opens up.

It's a perfect kiss.

Sweet, soft and sensual.

There is also absolutely no expectation that it will go further. He isn't ready for that. Even though I want to show him that I don't care about how he looks, that what I feel for him is *real*, he will bolt, and I will probably never see him again.

I sigh softly as our tongues twist around each other. I cup his face as I deepen it slightly, pressing my body against his.

Then, I pull away and climb off him, to lie next to him again. I take his hand and link our fingers, resting my head on his chest.

"You are so beautiful," he murmurs.

"So are you," I reply. I will keep telling him until he believes it.

"Have you figured out why Hell has frozen over?" he asks after a heavy pause.

"It has to do with Shax, I know it," I say. "Do you know where he is?"

"Sort of," he replies carefully.

"Meaning?" I ask, just as carefully.

"He isn't in Hell, nor the Wasteland. He isn't on Earth, nor in Heaven."

"Then where the fuck is he?" I ask, probably harsher than I meant to. I sit up and give him an apologetic look.

"It's a midway place," he says, ignoring my outburst.

"Midway between where?"

"Earth and Heaven," he says, his pale eyes searching mine.

"Are you fucking kidding me?" I shriek, leaping off the bed and pacing around the room like a caged tiger. "Damn you, Shax! You fucking traitor!" I sweep my hand over everything on the dresser and it goes flying off to the side.

Sid sits up quickly, scooting off the bed to crush himself into the corner of the room furthest away from me, his knees up against his chest. "Don't be too hasty to judge," he whispers.

I grab a hold of my temper quicker than I have in history. Gregory will be proud.

"I'm sorry, Sid," I say quietly. "Please, don't be afraid of me. I won't ever hurt you."

He nods, but he doesn't remove himself from the corner.

I clench my fists, digging my sharp nails into my palms. "Tell me what you know."

"Not much. Just a vague feeling of this place. I don't know where it is. He is struggling with a decision that is weighing on him." He scrunches up his face. "It's difficult. Painful…"

"Hey," I say, approaching him as quickly as I dare. I drop to my knees in front of him and put my hands on his knees. "You don't have to do this. I will find him another way."

"But this helps you. I want to help you. I want to have a use…"

"Oh, Sid. You don't need to have a use. That's not why I want you. Your being here is enough for me. We can take this as slowly as you are comfortable with."

"He is tormented," he whispers. It's strained and I hate what this is doing to him. "He has a choice to make."

"Between Hell and Heaven," I say bitterly, slumping my shoulders. "He is part Angel. I should've expected this. But I thought he was happy here. Well, as happy as he could be. Have I done this to him? Is it my fault that he left me to see if the other side was a better choice for him?"

"I don't know," Sid says quietly. "I can't read that much from him. I can try harder."

"No, you don't need to, my love. Rest now. You have done more than enough. Thank you." I stroke his face with the back of my hand.

I am aching to Shift and destroy. I am holding onto it for dear life so as not to scare this fragile male in front of me.

My stomach is churning, I feel nauseous. The brand on my mound is burning like the fires of Hell, but I smile at him and kiss him softly.

His twisted lips form a smile of understanding. "Go and do what you need to do. I will find a room and be here when you need me."

"I will always need you," I whisper and kiss him again. The need to force him to service me to get rid of the fury that has built up is now strong. But I can't do that to him. I need to find a male, or two, who will fuck the rage out of me, and I know just where to start.

I stand up and with a final smile at Sid, I flame out of Shax's room to the one male that I already know can get this job done and do it well.

CHAPTER 6

Killian

I HAVEN'T MOVED since Annabelle left and the other males filtered out of the Dining Hall. I have been contemplating my future if she goes ahead and walks the Earth. It will be catastrophic for Earth if the Four Horsemen are called to converge in one place all at the same time. We will be brought to her by her power as the Anti-Christ and I will be the one to step forward and start the Apocalypse. It's all very well in theory, but the reality of that is something that makes my blood run cold.

Will I survive in a war against Heaven's elite? I don't have an answer for that. A few days ago I couldn't have cared less – it is what I was made for, after all – now, after agreeing to be with Annabelle, things have changed.

I have changed.

The connection that I have to her is, in a word, startling.

I smile as I feel the tingling burn of the 'A' on the back of my neck. I touch it and hiss as it fires up. My smile turns to a small chortle as I remember her face when I did the same to her. She was *livid*. However, if she was really that pissed off about it now, she would have fired back at me. I wasn't surprised at all that the mark stayed imprinted on her skin, so is the depth of our connection. She is Hell and I am bound to this place.

Bound to *her*.

As soon as she started talking about Axelle being Luc's Demon Bound, I knew that it pertained to me.

Anna has absolutely no idea and I hope to keep it that way for as long as possible. She spoke about the trials, but I don't think that is necessary for us. All the rules have changed with her being a female. A strong, beautiful female. I have enjoyed pushing her boundaries today, but I will no longer. I tested her this morning by sitting at the head of the table to see if she would capitulate or put me in my place. I couldn't have been prouder by her response. She has surprised me with her ferocity and loyalty, but also her ability to love. I came back here knowing she was in power and it disappointed me. I watched her grow up as an entitled little Hellcat with a temper that could shake the Earth's foundations. Yes, she is still prone to an outburst, but I would no longer call them tantrums. She has worked really hard to mature and learn how to control her temper. I see that Gregory is a significant part of that and his role here is welcomed and clear. I will certainly not stand in the way of a deeper relationship between them, but the human has a long way to go before he is ready to accept Annabelle and Hell for eternity, in spite of what he thinks.

I stand up, deciding to find Elijah. He has been gone for too long and I'm worried that Darius has managed to bring him down for breaking the lockdown. He is a stubborn fool, but he cares about the Hounds, and that is the way it should be.

With a crack of lightning, I transport myself to the

kennels and Elijah, only to be slapped in the face with a scene that not only turns me on immensely, but also makes me growl at the stench of blood, *her* blood, splattered all over the floor.

"Elijah," I snarl at the Master of Hellhounds, as Annabelle rides him hard in the middle of the doorway. She has the lintel in a white-knuckled grip, using it to leverage herself up and down on Elijah's dick as he savagely bites her neck, scraping his claws down her arms. He is partial way through a Shift to his Hellhound form and while the sight of the Demon Queen fucking him in his natural state is something I would dearly love to see, he is fucking hurting her, and that is not acceptable.

He ignores me as he continues to chew on her. She writhes around and then shudders violently, coming all over his cock, making him groan in response.

Fuck. I'm all sorts of turned on right now.

"Stop being such a pussy and get over here," Annabelle pants. "He isn't doing anything I don't want him to."

She hauls herself up again, tearing his fangs out of her neck, this time high enough to get her legs over his shoulders so that he can eat her out. He grips her thighs as he buries his face between her legs. She leans back so that she falls upside down while he holds onto her in a fucking delicious acrobatic move that makes me step forward.

"You are fucking gorgeous," I murmur down to her and unzip my pants.

She laughs, a wicked sound that makes my dick bounce.

Elijah flips her over, gripping her hips to keep her steady as she lowers her feet to the floor. She rests her hand on my thigh and takes me in her mouth.

"Fuck," I groan, making eye contact with Elijah.

He holds my gaze, his yellow eyes intense with holding off on a full shift and the heat of the moment.

"Fuck her ass," I murmur to him.

She pulls her mouth off me and lets Elijah lead her to the bed. She gets on all fours with him behind her. He parts her cheeks and spits on her asshole before guiding his dick roughly inside her. She yelps as he tears her open, but she doesn't stop him.

Even though it's obvious she wants this, I say, "You're a fucking beast."

"She loves it," he replies.

I can't argue with that. Her eyes are alight with Hellfire and it speaks to the darkest part of me. There are places that I want to go with her that no normal Demon would've even thought about. I want to fuck her while she is in her natural Demonic form, her wings flapping behind her as I pound into her.

I grab my cock and guide it back into her mouth. "I want to come all over your face and make you dirty, little whore," I whisper to her.

Her moan is muffled by my enormous dick in her mouth.

"Pull her back, I want to fuck her pussy," I say to Elijah. "I want to see the mark that makes that cunt mine."

She hisses as Elijah pulls her back and off my cock. He keeps his dick inside her ass, falling back to the bed with her on top of him.

She opens her legs wider, daring me to touch her. I reach out and run the back of my fingers over the 'K' imprinted on her delicate skin.

"My cunt," I say to her, pushing my finger against her clit. "Say it."

"Your cunt," she answers back. I wasn't sure she would, but she said she'd defer to me when we fuck, so I'm pleased with her response.

I flick her clit and then lean forward, resting my foot on the bed as I slide into her dripping wet hole.

She throws her head back in rapture as I start to pound into her.

"Look at you, you filthy bitch," I say quietly. "A dick up your cunt and one up your ass and you still aren't happy, are you? You want more."

"Yes," she pants, which only makes me fuck her harder. It only makes Elijah impale her ass on his dick harder and faster. "More. More!"

"What about a pussy on your lips? Do you want that, slut?"

Her eyes flash with danger, but she smiles at me. "Yes," she says defiantly. "I want to tongue fuck a pussy while you fuck me with your dick."

I stifle my groan. The visual is hot as fuck, but I see now that Annabelle is going to let Xavi pursue her. She will take Xavier to her bed and there isn't a damn thing any of us will be able to do about it. My fellow Horseman is not my first choice as another lover for her. I accept that she needs more, but Xavier isn't the one she should choose. Not the least because of the effect it will have on *me* being in such close proximity to *her*. It's not even remotely sexual. I wouldn't touch Pestilence with a thousand-foot barge pole, but the consequences of two Horsemen being in such close quarters will be severe for us all.

I doubt that Annabelle will care though. She will see it as a challenge to overcome.

"Harder," she screams at us. "More!"

We give her what she wants, brutally fucking her until she comes all over my cock in a climax that goes on and on.

When she clenches around me for the fifth time, I lose it. I pull out and aim my dick at her face, splashing my cum all over her mouth, cheeks and eyes.

"That's it, baby. Now you're all dirty," I murmur to her and bend over to kiss her deeply.

She pushes me back and grins at me, just as Elijah shoots his load into her ass.

"Now you," she murmurs.

I wait for Elijah to move over to me. I won't go to him. He will see to me, not the other way around while our Queen watches us.

He shuffles over, a look of lust heating his eyes. He bends down and grips my still-hard cock in his hand. His mouth closes over my tip and I groan, closing my eyes and letting my head fall back while I enjoy the feel of his hot mouth work expertly over my stiff shaft. It jerks in his mouth eager for more, eager for a thick stream of cum to coat his tongue and slide down his throat.

"Yes, E," I grunt, thrusting my hips forward.

Annabelle moans softly. "Can I touch you?" she whispers.

I open my eyes to see her riveted to Elijah's mouth fucking me with the vigor of the beast he is.

I nod, knowing that she is talking to me.

She reaches out to cup my balls, squeezing gently. I let out a soft groan which encourages her to squeeze harder.

She lets me go moments before I'm about to burst my load and stands up to kiss me. She swishes her tongue against mine and then pulls away with a sultry smile. "Fuck him, War. Fuck his ass so hard, he screams. I want to suck him off while you do it."

"You don't get to dictate our fucking," I chide her, roughly grabbing her throat. "Elijah has a fantasy that he wants to fulfil, don't you, *puppy*?"

He pulls his mouth off me and nods.

"What is it?" Annabelle asks as I fling her back to the bed and Elijah scoots next to her, shoving his huge dick in her mouth.

"Suck him off, slut," I order her. "Before he comes, he

wants to slide into your slick pussy and fuck your cunt while I fuck his ass."

"Uhnnn," she moans around Elijah's meat stuffed into her mouth.

I stroke Elijah's head, treating him like the puppy she calls him.

He sighs happily as Annabelle licks, sucks and grazes her teeth over him.

The sight of her with her mouth full of dick sends a bolt of pure lust driving through me. I pull Elijah away and he falls between her legs, entering her swiftly and without hesitation.

"Yes!" she screams, taking his entire length in one deep thrust. "Fuck, yes."

I take that as my cue to grab the lube and work his asshole until it's ready to take me.

He braces himself as he feels my tip pushing against the tight hole. I find his rhythm and thrust into him at the same time as he draws back from Annabelle, slamming my hips against him as I bury myself balls deep in his ass.

"Fuck," he growls, feeling every inch of me fill him up as he fills up Annabelle's cunt.

He thrusts into her again, but I stay still, letting him work his ass fucking as well as getting his dick coated with Annabelle's cunt juice.

"Ah," she cries out, desperately looking over Elijah's shoulder by propping herself up on her elbows. "Oh, yeah, that is fucking hot. Fuck him hard."

I grab his hips and take control of the rhythm, my eyes never leaving hers. It doesn't take me long to feel my climax start to build. My balls are aching, my shaft throbbing as Elijah pounds her pussy until his ass cheeks clench and he spurts his load into her with a loud grunt. I thrust one last time and fill his ass with my cum as Annabelle bites her bottom lip seductively, coming hard as she watches me.

The second I withdraw from Elijah, she wipes me down and then has my dick in her filthy, slutty mouth, arousing me further and fucking me so hard with it, it feels like she is going to suck my dick right off.

"That right, dirty whore. Service me with that slutty mouth," I murmur to her.

Elijah gets to work on her clit with his fingers until she moans from her release and then I come again, panting heavily. I have the stamina to fuck her a thousand times but having so many orgasms in such a short space of time has taken its toll on me. It's never happened to me before and will take only the two creatures with me now for it to happen again.

"Thanks, boys," Annabelle says, crawling over to the side of the bed, leaving us panting from the effort of trying to please her. "That did the trick."

She stretches her back out, her arms high above her head.

I give Elijah a curious look. "Demon Queen rage," he mutters.

"Oh, really?" I ask her. "You fuck away the Shift? With him? Why didn't you come to me?" I am slightly hurt and extremely glad that I happened upon this healing scene.

"I know he gets the job done right," she says with a shrug, indicating her neck and arms. "He knows what I need to release the tension."

"I see," I murmur. "Come to me next time, Princess. I have ideas that I would love to share with you."

She gives me a sultry smile. "You're on, War. Now, if you will excuse me. Someone has been banging at the door to the residence for ten minutes now. I'd better go and see who it is before Darius decides enough is enough."

Elijah and I exchange a puzzled look. How did she hear

that from here? I suppose maybe it's not about hearing it but sensing it instead. The residence was created from her power. She is connected to it.

"We'll catch up with you later," I say before stooping down to give her a kiss on her forehead.

She flames out and I turn to Elijah, fury in my eyes. "Ravage her again that way and I will kick your ass so hard, you will feel it for a century," I snarl at him.

"So protective, Lian," he teases me, walking over to pick up his discarded clothes and pulling his shirt back over his head. "Who'd have thought?" He gives me a knowing look as I glower at him.

I have no answer for that.

CHAPTER 7

Annabelle

I LAND in front of the double doors to the residence, irritated. I wasn't quite done with Elijah and Killian, but this incessant knocking was getting on my nerves. It echoes through my head, making it hard to ignore.

I plump up my tits, squashed into a tight black corset and fluff out my hair.

Reaching for both of the door handles, I ceremoniously open the doors together, stepping back and resting my hands on the edges of the doors.

"Yes?" I inquire.

I take in Pestilence standing on my doorstep in an ice-blue cloak covering her from head to toe.

"My Queen," she says. "How kind of you to let me in." She barges inside, forcing me to take a step back or be barreled over.

"Do come in," I murmur, shutting the doors. "By the way, you do know that there is a lockdown on, don't you?"

"Hmm? Oh, that. Sure," she says idly looking around the foyer before her blue eyes land on me.

I raise my eyebrow at her. She doesn't give a flying shit that Darius would throw her in the pit if he caught her outside.

"Darius could suck your essence from your body before you knew what hit you," I point out. "And I hear that he is *real* hungry right now."

"Oh, he wishes," she scoffs. "How about that drink?"

"I've already read your report," I lie but I'm talking to her back. She is already walking away from me and deep into the residence.

Pursing my lips at having to follow her, I flame out and back in next to her, grabbing her arm and then taking her to the sin bin.

"Oh, I've heard of this place," she comments.

"Well, it's normally a bit more fun," I reply, gesturing to the empty room. "But you get the idea."

"Indeed," she murmurs, running her hand over a nearby rack. The one where Killian fucked me like a filthy whore and then told me he would be with me.

I shiver at the memory and sit down in an armchair with another one turned towards it.

"Sit," I order Xavier.

She turns back towards me and walks over to sit down. She flicks her hood back and crosses her legs. I take in the expanse of naked thigh right up to her exposed tits as the cloak falls away.

"Do you usually turn up uninvited and naked?" I ask her.

"Not usually," she drawls. "But in this case, I wanted to make an impression. Killian is quite difficult to see around," she adds with a small laugh.

"Oh, you don't need to tell me," I murmur. "Stand up."

She does as I instruct and pulls on the tie at her neck,

letting the cloak fall completely away from her. I enjoy looking at her for a moment. She has long, lean legs, a shaven mound, slender hips, flat stomach, tits that are about a handful with pretty pink nipples.

"You are attracted to your fellow Horseman?" I inquire with only a bit of bite.

The look she gives me would make me laugh if we weren't talking about one of *my* males.

"No," she states with conviction. "I don't like dick. I'm strictly a tits and pussy female."

"No dick, huh?" I ask, scrunching up my nose. "Not even a strap-on?"

She shakes her head. "Nope."

"Huh," I mutter.

"You've seen mine, you going to show me yours?" she asks, leaning over me and resting her hands on the arm of the chair.

I narrow my eyes at her. "I don't give it up in the first ten minutes," I lie again.

She chuckles. "I find that hard to believe. Something tells me you take what you want, when you want it."

"And?"

"You want me," she whispers, reaching out to pull the laces on the front of my corset.

I don't stop her. I let her entwine her fingers into the laces and pull back her hand to loosen them.

The corset opens up enough for my tits to be partially exposed.

Xavier licks her lips, her eyes taking in the sight.

"You're pretty sure of yourself," I remark. I sit back, crossing my legs, propping my elbow on the arm of the chair and resting my fingers under my chin.

"I go after what I want," she says confidently, kneeling in front of me and once again reaching for the corset. She pulls the sides away so that my tits are now completely on show. She circles my nipples with her fingers, tracing lightly, making me shiver. Her skin is as icy as the snow outside. My hot skin almost sizzles under her feather light touches.

When I don't bat her away, she leans forward, squeezing one of my nipples and then sucking it into her mouth.

I can't help the gasp that escapes my lips.

It's like my nipple is encased in an ice cube. It peaks painfully, as does the other one which she pinches roughly between her cold fingers.

Xavier flicks my nipple one last time with her tongue and then pulls away with a wicked smile. "Want me to carry on?"

Wordlessly, I uncross my legs and undo the button on my leather pants. I sit back as she lowers the zipper and slides her hand inside.

"Mmm," I murmur as her fingers find my clit and she circles it gently.

"*Ahna*," Drescal says, appearing next to me and looking down at Xavier with her hand in my pants. I feel like I've been caught doing something wrong and it spikes my blood to rush to my clit and thud under her fingers as I let out a muffled moan.

She pulls her hand back with a smug smile and stands up.

If she expected Drescal to look at her, she would be disappointed. He doesn't tear his eyes away from me.

"Put your cloak back on," I say to her, holding Drescal's gaze.

I see her out of the corner of my eye bend down to do as I say. As soon as she has covered up, Drescal turns to her with a smile. "Xavier, nice to see you again."

"And you," she replies. She gives me a cool smile that belies the fire in her eyes. She bows her head briefly. "My Queen. I'll leave you two alone."

She saunters off and I call over my shoulder, "Find yourself a room, Pestilence. There's a lockdown on, don't you know."

I hear her soft snort of amusement and grin to myself as she wiggles her fingers at me.

"Door's open," Drescal calls after her as I turn back towards him.

"New player?" he asks, taking my hand and linking our fingers together.

"Maybe," I say slowly. "You got a problem with that?"

"Not at all," he says smoothly, pulling me up.

He sits and drags me onto his lap.

I lean forward and kiss him. His hands go to my backside to pull me closer, making me rub my pussy over the bulge in his pants.

"Forgive me?" he asks, breaking our kiss.

"Guess so," I murmur.

"Good," he says with a smirk, gripping my chin. "I know you want me for the seduction, but… fuck me?"

I giggle and nod, kissing him again, still riled up from my near Shift and Xavier's attention. It also reminds me of Shax's betrayal, which starts the circle all over again. Gripping Dres's shirt, I kiss him fiercely only to be interrupted moments later by an unwanted visitor.

"Pardon me, Your Majesty," Roberta says, having popped in next to us.

I give her a steely-eyed glare. "What?" I snap.

"You need to come with me. Now!" she says, gripping my arm. Without waiting for me to do up my corset, or my pants, she transports us back to her headquarters, where we land in front of a scene that awakens the beast and no amount of counting *or* fucking is going to stop *Her* from coming out.

CHAPTER 8

Devlin

I SIT *at the dive in the worst part of Hell and drown my sorrows. At the very least, I'm trying. It's not working very well. Being a powerful Demon will do that to you though. It'll stunt your ability to get so fucking pissed, you forget your own name.*

"'Nother," I drawl at the barkeep. He does me a solid and slides the whole bottle over. "Ta," I mutter.

I pour out a vodka for me and another for my fallen. I down them both quickly and pour them out again. "For you, Pierre."

I sigh and slump forward. Pierre. My favorite apprentice. A human so special, his aura glowed around him a perfect black, telling me he would be perfect for me to turn into a Necromancer and carry on Hell's work by my side, until he was ready to fly on his own. Too bad I'd gotten on the wrong side of a collection of Voodoo practitioners who took him a day after I turned him, to punish me. Without me to guide him through the process and offer him my blood to drink, he withered away and died. For real.

I won't say that I'm sentimental by any stretch of the imagination, but this has hit me hard.

45

He was special.

Not just because of his destiny, but because I cared about him as much as a Demon could.

I barely look up as the door sweeps open to let in the scorching putrid air that permeates this part of Hell's center.

"Ugh!" a female's voice resounds around the bar. "Hellpit flies!"

"That's what happens when you slum it this close to the pits, sweetheart," I drawl.

"Humph," she mutters and saunters over to me. She sits and regards me.

I look up into startling green eyes, taking in her fiery hair, and slender body with a rack that I want to bury my head in between. She is wearing a black leather dress with a zipper which is holding it together at the front, pulled down enough to give me a good view of her cleavage. No doubt a newbie Seductress recalled from Earth to report in. Sure fucking looks like it and those bitches aren't usually my thing.

"Not interested," I comment and turn back to my drink. As much as I'd like to hit that, I'm just really not in the mood. Not right now. Not when the last being I fucked was Pierre right before I killed him and turned him to follow in my footsteps.

"Who says I am?" she retorts and snaps her fingers at the bartender. "Whatever he's having," she adds to him.

He brings her two vodkas and I snort in amusement. She downs them and asks for more. She is going to be on her ass in next to no time. There is no way that anyone who looks like that is any kind of powerhouse around here. She is a lightweight looking for a bump up, probably.

"How about we take this to a booth?" she asks and gets up, taking her two new drinks with her.

Like a dickhead, I follow her. Maybe a quick fuck in a public place is just the way to go.

I slide in next to her and watch her down the vodka. She takes the bottle from me and places it to those full lips, gulping back half of it as if it is water.

I chuckle. She is entertaining me and getting my head out of my arse for a few moments.

Twenty minutes later, she is writhing around on my lap, kissing me with a passion that makes my dick so hard, it's painful. I drag on her arse to get her closer so that she can rub up against me.

I pull away from her, lowering her zipper to catch sight of those magnificent tits when a thought occurs to me. "What's your name, sweetheart?"

She laughs provocatively. "Hell's Belle, baby," she purrs at me and my blood runs cold.

What a fucking arsehole.

I grab her around her waist and dump her on the seat next to me, scooting across the booth to escape from her clutches.

"Are you fucking kidding?" I snap at her. "Do you want me to die a painful death?"

She rolls those pretty eyes at me and takes another shot of vodka. "Stop being such a pussy," she drawls.

"Pussy?" I roar at her. "If your father knew you were in here, if he knew you were in here wriggling around all over my dick, he would string me up by it and peel my skin off with a potato peeler!"

Un-fucking-believable that I fell for her smoky eyes and sassy attitude. Okay, and her massive rack.

"What's a potato peeler?" she asks, scrunching up her nose.

I blink at her. "What? Ugh, never mind. You need to leave. Now." I point to the door and she laughs at me.

"What a prude. Thought you were up for it," she says, leaping up onto the table and giving me an exceptionally good view of her long legs.

I shudder at the thought of what sits at the top of them. I was about to stick my dick into the Devil's daughter. "What a prick," I mutter under my breath. "How old are you anyway?" She can be no older than sixteen, if I recall.

"Seventeen," she says, giving me a lingering look, and pulls the zipper holding her dress together, all the way down to her navel.

I can't help but look at her tits. Two luscious mounds with ripe, peaked nipples that I moan at.

"Come and get it boys!" she calls out, her eyes still on me.

There isn't a Demon in the dive that ignores her request. A couple of dozen hands reach for her to her delight, but no, it's not happening while I'm standing here. I like my life. Love it even. Okay, so yeah, the last few days have been rough as shit, but no way am I giving the Devil a chance to blame me for his daughter's gangbang in this disgusting place.

I jump up on the table with her and grab her arm. I whirl us out of the bar and straight to the door of the residence.

She gives me a look that tells me that I fell for her ploy and now she has me right where she wants me. She grabs my black leather coat and drags me towards her, kissing me with those lips, that tongue which is making my knees weak.

"Fuck, I can't do this," I groan, stepping back from her.

"Oh, but you can," she says. "I chose you."

"Chose me for what?" I ask confused. I think the vodka is finally hitting home, along with her sensual kisses, I'm feeling a bit addled.

"To take my virginity," she states so decisively, I think I've misheard her.

"Come again?" I ask, raising my eyebrow at her.

She doesn't answer me, just grabs me and flames us to her bedroom. Panic doesn't cover the feeling that radiates through me.

"No!" I say, holding my hand up. "Not a fucking chance, sweetheart."

"Don't be scared of my dad. He won't even know."

"Of course he will! He is the Devil for fuck's sake!"

"Stop being such a pus..."

"If you call me a pussy one more time, I will batter yours with my dick and not be a gentleman about it," I growl at her, fists clenched.

She laughs in my face.

Fucking bitch.

She has captured my attention that's for damn sure. I acted out of self-preservation by bringing her back home but now...I am falling like a fool for her.

"Tell you what," I say, changing tactic and putting my smooth, sexy, gets-their-knickers-wet swagger on. "I will bust your cherry on one condition."

"You're negotiating with me?" she asks incredulously, folding her arms over her chest.

"I am, sweetheart. I'll do what you want me to do, but we do it my way, in my time. I want to have a bit of fun with you first. I want to take you out about Hell, have a few drinks, get to know you first."

"What?" she asks, a puzzled frown falling over her gorgeous face. "You want to date me?"

"Not exactly," I scoff, although if she hadn't thought the idea was so ludicrous, then maybe. "I just don't want to be that guy you forget after I give you what you want."

Her eyes light up. "Oh, I see. You want to be remembered, forever etched in my memory."

"Somethin' like that, darlin."

"Your accent is cute," she says, throwing me off guard. "You sound like Johnny Rotten."

"You know who the Sex Pistols are but not what a potato peeler is?" I ask with a laugh. She is an absolute delight.

She shrugs. "Mom prefers to focus on certain things."

"Oh?" I'm intrigued.

She sits back, happy to talk. "Yeah, she likes us to watch the films and keeps us up to date on music and the news and stuff. She wants us to know Earth as well as she does."

"Hmm," I murmur and sit down to let her regale me with all the things she knows. She is fascinating and her vivacity is a major turn on.

"We have a deal," she interrupts herself a few moments later. "You be the one to take my virginity and I'll let you do it your way."

"Deal," I say immediately with a slow smile that she definitely appreciates.

"Dev!"

Slam.

"Dev, wake up you asshole," Drescal's voice echoes through my head.

I open my eyes to find myself staring into the pages of the book I was reading when I must've fallen asleep. It is resting on my face and is whipped off a second later as I blink to adjust.

"Dante's Inferno?" he scoffs.

"It's a classic," I mutter, sitting up and trying to get my raging hard-on to go down. I'd been dreaming about Annabelle again and our first meeting. It's a regular thing, sometimes the same as with this dream, but sometimes with different endings. It always ends with us fucking but this time I was rudely interrupted. "What do you want?" I add.

He flings the book on the nightstand. "Do you think Anna has a ninth circle for those who betray?" he muses.

"Is that what you fucking came in here for?" I snap.

"She has fire cubes."

Drescal and I exchange a look at the voice that filtered through the wall. "What?" I shout back.

"Fire cubes. Downstairs for the ones she deems the worst offenders."

"Who is that?" I mouth to Drescal.

He shrugs.

I climb off the bed and head towards the door. Drescal follows me. I push open the door next to the room I'd picked out and walk inside.

I see a tragically scarred male sitting on the bed with his legs up, his knees against his chest and his arms wrapped around them. The Night Mare.

"Sid, right?" I ask, coming in a bit further, Drescal peering over the top of my head. I'm not a short man, so this pisses me off.

He nods. "Sorry. I'm very sensitive to sound waves. I could hear you talking."

"That's okay," I say gently. He is like a scared rabbit. Not that I blame him. He looks like he has been through a trauma that none of us would find fun.

"Annabelle told me to find a room. This was the first one I came across that was empty," he says.

"That's good," I say. "I know she wants you to stick around."

"H-how do you know that?" he stammers.

"I saw the way she looked at you in her bedroom yesterday. After Shax."

He blinks his pale eyes.

"I know her face well," I add.

"I know her face too," he says. "She is pretty."

"Very," I agree and nudge Drescal to stop standing there like an arsehole with his dick in his hand.

"Gorgeous," he murmurs, getting the hint.

I'm trying to make this Demon feel safe. Annabelle wants him here and it's the least we can do to help. Ignoring him won't accomplish that.

"You love her. You all love her," Sid says. "Does she love you?"

Drescal and I exchange another look. "Erm," I say. "She…"

"There are what? Like seven of us now and she hasn't said

51

that to any of us," Drescal says.

"How do you know?" I ask him, also sitting down.

"I think she would have said it once to someone, if she were so inclined, while we were fucking," he points out.

"Oh, good point," I mutter.

"She says she wants to love me, but that I have to let her," Sid says quietly.

"Well, you are a lucky fucker. I haven't even had that from her, and I've known her for years," I say with a smile.

"Why won't you let her?" Drescal asks.

I kick the leg of his chair and give him a look.

"I don't trust that what she says is true," Sid mutters.

"If there's one thing I know about Annie, it's that she never says shit she doesn't mean when it comes to her emotions. It's hard for her to express her vulnerable side," I say.

"Oh," Sid says and drops his knees, sitting cross-legged now that he feels more at ease with us, I guess. "So, I should let her in?"

I nod encouragingly.

He nods back and shoots me a small smile.

"We'll leave you to think about that," I say and stand up. I still want to know what got Drescal's knickers in a twist that he came bursting into my room.

"Okay," Sid says, shyly. "Thank you."

"Anytime," I reply and leave with Drescal following me.

As I shut the door behind me, I turn to Drescal. "What did you come and find me for?"

"Oh, that," he says, shaking his head. "Seems our Queen has chosen another chess piece."

"Oh?" I ask with a frown, finding his metaphor surprising but accurate. "Who?"

"You will shoot your load off when I tell you," he says with a smirk.

"Who?" I demand, getting slightly concerned now.

"Pestilence," he says smugly.

"Fucking fuck," I breathe out. "*Two* Horsemen? What is she trying to do to us?"

"Fucked if I know, but I saw them together and there is no way she will back down from Xavi. There is something there that is explosive."

"Explosive about sums it up. Does Killian know about this?" I ask.

He shrugs. "Don't know, but is it up to us to go and tell him?" he asks a rather damn good question.

Personally, while not "afraid" of the Horseman of War, giving him the news that he will be sharing Annabelle with his fellow Apocalypse harbinger is not something that I want to do. It seems that Drescal is of the same mind, so I focus on the bit that gets me excited.

"A female, hmm?" I murmur. "I do like seeing her lick pussy while I fuck her ass."

"Knew it would turn you on," Drescal says with a laugh. "So, you're okay with Xavier becoming her lover?" He has turned serious.

I shrug. "Not up to me. Not only was I last in the door, but this is Annie's show. I will do whatever it is she wants me to do."

"Yeah," Drescal says, with a slow nod. "Same."

I find his response a little odd, but don't call him on it. He is probably just trying to get his head around it. Bringing a female into our circle could cause complications for him being what he is, but *not* in this case. I've known Xavi a long time. She doesn't do dick. I'm not worried about her and Drescal. I *am* worried about her and Killian. Catastrophic consequences are the two words that come to mind.

However, I've come to learn that life with Annabelle Pandora is *never* boring.

CHAPTER 9

Annabelle

"Get your hands off him!" I roar, knowing that the Shift is descending, and I can't stop it.

I see Aleister on his knees, a chain around his neck and his arms behind his back in Darius's grip as he looms over him, keeping *my* Master Gargoyle down.

"Darius," I growl, my voice changing, going deeper as I start to Shift. My wings sprout out and Roberta ducks out of reach. I'm not in full Devil mode or I would kill everyone, including Aleister. But this is enough to satisfy the craving that hasn't been put to rest since I found out about Shax's trip to mid-Heaven.

"He broke lockdown," Darius rasps. "He belongs in the dungeon with all of the other offenders."

"No, he belongs in the sky, looking out for the residence," I snarl back, my tail swishing wildly. It's a good thing that I was practically naked anyway when I arrived here uncere-moniously. I barely had any clothes to burst out of. "His Gargoyles are the eyes up there. They are *his* subjects."

"Broke lockdown," Darius snaps, his big square head finally rising to look at me. I don't know what Dad was thinking when he created this beast. He is hideous to look at. He has two rows of spikes running along the sides of his head, a wide mouth with several rows of sharp teeth. He stands over seven feet tall on his big-ass feet and his skin is made from dark gray scales with a green tinge to it, hard enough to be his armor.

"He was never supposed to be locked down in the first place," I argue, getting even more riled up the longer we stand here. "Let. Him. Up."

With a low rumble, Darius gives Aleister a rough shove, but lets him go.

Aleister gives me a brief smile as he gets to his feet. He keeps his distance, knowing that he can't get too close to me.

"You get one," Darius grits out. "The next one is mine."

"Not if they belong to me," I inform him. "Ask Roberta who is off limits." I turn to her and give her a nod of thanks.

She gives me a bland look back, but deep down I know she appreciates it. Bitch. She might be a monstrosity, but it's nice to see she has my back...or rather, the back of my lover.

I give her another look. She is trying not to look at Aleister but can't resist it seems.

I snort and look at the Gargoyle. He doesn't have a fucking clue that Roberta has the hots for him. What a riot. I'm going to enjoy seeing him blush when I tell him.

"You're all dismissed," I grate. It's starting to hurt talking in this form.

Darius and his security men leave under a cloud. Aleister gestures upwards to me with his hand and I give him a nod. Roberta breaks the chain and he hightails it out of the office as I concentrate on getting the Shift to start so that I can go and be with my lover without frying him to a crisp.

With a roar that tears through me as painfully as the Shift,

I suddenly find myself standing starkers in the office with Roberta. She gives me a once-over, which I do nothing to stop. She should look at me. Everyone should see me naked at least once and either want to be me or fuck me.

Hopefully, Roberta is thinking she wants to be me. If she wanted to fuck, I'd have to say thanks but no way.

I snap my fingers, covering up and then I flame out of the office to the roof where Aleister is waiting for me, with nothing but a smile on his face.

"Oh?" I ask, approaching him slowly. "You expecting something?"

"Only if you're offering," he says with a laugh. "But no, I have to get back out there. Darius was pretty annoying in keeping me delayed as much as possible."

Annoying isn't the word *I'd* use, but it fits Aleister's mild manner perfectly. "So, this is for a Shift? How disappointing," I murmur, moving in closer.

"Thanks for rescuing me." He gives me another laugh. "Words I never thought I'd say."

"Anytime," I say breezily but then give him a fierce frown. "Actually, scrap that. Don't get caught again."

"I'll try not to," he says, wrapping his arms around me and giving me a kiss.

"Keep that up and I'll have to delay you even more," I say, stepping back.

"I'll hold you to that later," he says and then Shifts. He hops up onto the roof ledge and then with a swoop of his huge wings, he's gone.

"Dammit, now I'm all riled up again," I complain. As soon as I think about what started all of this in the first place, my arousal plummets to the ground and keeps on going.

Shax.

How dare he do this to me. I'm going to have to go there and get him back by whatever means necessary. Only problem is, I really want to avoid going to Earth and starting its destruction before I am actually ready to bring forth Armageddon and secondly, there is no way I can get to mid-Heaven. I'm *all* Demon. There isn't a single Angelic bone in my body.

I do, however, know someone who does and I'm willing to bet my crown that he will want to get his son back from the clutches of the other side as much as I do and save me from threatening them to get my brother back.

Decision made, I head off to the wing of the residence where my mother and her husbands live. I clench my fists knowing that Shax has the box in which my father is, and he hasn't brought it to me yet. This level of betrayal is going to be difficult to get over. If I even can.

I knock at the door to my parent's place. "We need to talk," I say as soon as it opens. "Shit is hitting the fan all over the damned place."

"No fucking kidding," Mom drawls and opens the door wide to let me in. "Where do we start?"

CHAPTER 10

Aleister

I LAND GENTLY on the roof of the Rooftop, to Igor pacing fretfully.

"Finally!" he exclaims when he sees me. "I thought you were done for."

"Gee, thanks," I mutter, but give him a tight smile. "I'm fine. Annabelle sorted it out."

"Annabelle?" he inquires with a small smirk which then turns serious. He points upwards. "He shot you out of the fucking sky!" He points downwards, which probably indicates my plummet from several hundred feet.

"I'm fine," I reiterate, even though the pain in my side makes me want to weep. "Roberta fixed me and then Annabelle released me from arrest, so it's all good."

"You sure?" he asks, not sounding convinced.

"Yes. Oh, and keep the information about me being shot to yourself. If Annabelle finds out, she will eviscerate Darius and she needs him right now."

Igor nods slowly. "Okay," he says. "So, what now?"

"We get back to work. The change is due any minute now. We need to pull two from the south-east side to join the others at the pits. This change of climate, along with the lockdown, is going to cause trouble once the masses have worked themselves up enough."

"That leaves only two on the south-east side," Igor points out. "Is it enough?"

"It's the least active area right now, so we have to go where the hot spots are. Monty and Cliff will be fine on their own over there, and if need be, I can join them."

"Done," Igor says with a nod and leaves to deal with the changes.

Once he is gone, I slump into my desk chair and pull up my t-shirt. My side looks fine, so why the Hell is it hurting so bad?

"You need to tell her," Roberta says, popping in out of nowhere.

I give her a filthy look. "You healed me, what's the point?"

"I didn't heal you. I covered it up," she states and waves her hand over my torso.

"Fuck," I groan as the cover-up drops away and the wound reappears looking worse than it did before.

"You are a *Master* Gargoyle; I don't have the ability to heal you. She does."

"Then why not just tell her to begin with?" I snap.

"You know as well as I do that she would've eradicated Darius on the spot. She needs him right now, and quite frankly, so do I. I don't have the time to train up another Demon to take his place. Not to mention you saw the Shift. Do you really think that if she saw you on your knees bleeding out, she would've stopped there? We'd *all* be dead by now."

"Then how am I supposed to tell her now?" I ask with a baffled look at the ugly Demon.

"She will be calmer now. Perhaps," she says, avoiding my gaze.

"What you really mean is that you won't be there, so you'll be safe from her wrath," I drawl.

"You and she are lovers. She is less likely to Shift and kill you if you are by yourself."

"How thoughtful of you," I mutter. "What did he shoot me with anyway?" I ask after a beat.

"A dart made from the poison of a briar plant," she says.

"Oh," I say and give her a horrified look. "He's killing Demons."

"They shouldn't be breaking lockdown then, should they?" she says and disappears.

"Fuck," I mutter again. The briar plant is something that grows down in the marshes. Only the Swamp Demons are immune to it. It is lethal to every other fucker, including me it seems. There is no known cure for it.

"Great," I sigh and rub my hand over my face.

I have no choice but to tell Annabelle. I will be dead by the time night falls over her residence if I don't. I just hope that I can convince her to keep Darius alive. Something tells me that it isn't going to be an easy task and my strength is waning.

"Igor?" I call out softly. He will hear me wherever he is and come to me.

"Sir?" he asks a moment later. His eyes go wide when he sees the wound.

"I have to go to the residence. Call me if you need me."

He nods, his eyes not leaving the bleeding hole in my side. "I'll hold down the fort," he says. "And I won't say a word," he adds before I can threaten him not to.

"Thanks," I say and stand up.

Igor disappears and I walk slowly to the ledge of the roof.

I look down. Taking a deep breath, I Shift and flap my wings. I take off, but stumble slightly in the air.

I keep going, knowing that if I fall from the sky now, I'll be done for. I'm hanging onto the Shift for dear life. I only make it to the ground outside the residence before I Shift in midair against my will. I fall from the sky to the snow-covered ground, landing in a painful heap before I black out.

I come to with hushed voices whispering over me.

"You tell her."

"Fuck that. *You* tell her."

"Pah, ask the therapist to tell her. She's less likely to kill him."

I crack my eyes open and blink. I'm indoors on a bed, the pain in my side making me want to vomit.

Elijah and Killian are standing over me, debating on who gets to tell Annabelle about me, it seems.

"You're awake," Killian states. "Good. *You* can tell her."

"I planned on it. Just didn't make it," I rasp, my mouth bone dry. "Where is she?"

"Not sure," Elijah mutters. "Around somewhere. What the fuck happened to you?"

"Darius," I growl and try to sit up.

The pain radiates through my torso as the nausea sweeps its way across me. I groan and lie back down.

"Briar thorns?" Elijah asks.

"Yeah."

"Fucking asshole," he mutters.

"Make that two fucking assholes. Roberta knows about this," I inform them.

"Shit," Killian laughs. "Annabelle is going to have a field day with this."

"She can't kill him, or her. She needs them both."

Killian growls knowing that I'm right, but not wanting to concede.

"We need to find her. We can't help you," he states.

"Awesome. Get on that, would you. I'd like to tell her at least once that I love her before I'm eradicated," I grit out.

Killian breathes in deeply and says, "No need. She's here."

In the next second, she swoops into the room with her hair on fire. Like, literally. I've never seen anything like it before and probably never will again if she can't help me.

"WHAT THE FUCKING HELL?" she roars storming over to us.

Elijah scoots around to the other side of the bed to stand next to Killian. I, unfortunately, have nowhere to go.

"Who told you?" I ask, needing to know so that I can kill them if I survive. I wanted her calm and rational, not on fire and ready to annihilate everything that moves.

"No one," she spits out. "I can feel your pain. It's making me feel sick." She drops to her knees next to the bed and takes my hand, her fire-hair returning to normal, although still smoking a bit. "Who did this to you?"

"That isn't important. Can you heal me?"

"What is it?" she asks.

"Briar thorns," I whisper, my strength going rapidly now that she is here, and I can leave my life in her hands.

I see her exchange a fearful look with the other males.

"You can't save me," I say, resigned to my fate now that she is here. I can tell her what I need to. "I love you, Annabelle. You captured my heart the second I laid eyes on you. You have given me more happiness in the last few days than I have had in all my previous years combined…"

"Don't you fucking dare say goodbye to me, you fucking prick!" she screams in my face, tears of blood welling up in her eyes and spilling down her cheeks in a gory mess. "I will find a way. Just hang on, please, Aleister, just hang on."

"Okay," I mutter and close my eyes.

"Aleister!" She grips my shirt tightly. "Aleister!"

Darkness descends and her voice fades away.

CHAPTER 11

Shax

"I'M TAKING it back to Annabelle," I tell Vazna stoically.

Shadow was right. Flying, being free, gave me clarity. Annabelle is my main concern, my *only* concern with regard to this matter.

He gives me a tight smile. "Luc didn't want you to do that," he says stiffly.

"I know, but he isn't my father. He can't tell me to jump and I say how high. In fact, not even my father can do that," I add so that we are clear that I'm not a pushover in any aspect.

"You release Luc, you release Lucifer, is that what you want?" he asks earnestly. "I can assure you he will kill your sister to take back his power."

"You don't know that," I say. "Besides. He is my father's brother. If anyone can get through to Lucifer, it's his twin."

Shadow casts an amazed glance at me. Okay, so yeah, not exactly common knowledge around the Hell office fire pit but a fact, nonetheless.

"That is wishful thinking," Vazna murmurs.

"Look, I get that your side wants this done and dusted but it's not that simple for me," I snap at him.

"I understand. I do, Shax. Didn't you come to Earth seeking something other than your dark side? Didn't you want a chance to try out light?"

I frown at him. That's not what I'd wanted to do when I left Hell. I just wanted to see if there was a chance that light was in me and if being away from Hell would make that shine brighter than the darkness.

"We do things for the greater good. Luc understood that. It's why he came to me, knowing that you'd follow."

"He took a gamble," I say. "If I didn't come to Earth, no harm, no foul. The box would remain sealed."

"The box needs to be destroyed!" he suddenly shouts at me, finally losing the cool exterior that he has presented to me since we met.

"No," I state with conviction. Even if I hadn't already decided, his attitude would have been the clincher. "I hold all the cards here. You need me to destroy the box. I'm refusing. I'm taking it back to Hell so that Annabelle can open it and deal with the consequences."

"So you will leave her to handle it?" he scoffs.

"It's her responsibility, not mine. *My* responsibility is to remain loyal to her."

"That is your final decision?" he asks.

"Yes," I say, folding my arms.

"Then you leave me no choice." He waves his hand over Shadow.

She screams, a look of torment on her face. He is banishing her.

"No!" I shout out, reaching for her, but it's too late. Heaven's Guardian has banished a Demon back to Hell. She could arrive back anywhere, and with Hell being locked down, she is as good as dead.

"You bastard!" I shout, going for him.

He holds his hand up and I stop.

I growl at him, clenching my fists. "You've just killed her."

"Not my problem. My problem is that box and you refusing to destroy it. If you think banishing a Demon back to the fire pits is the only way I can hurt you, think again."

"Fucker!"

"You will destroy that box, Shax. Believe me when I say that."

"You can't keep me here," I grit out. "I'm a resident of Hell. It's against the laws."

"So, you've made your choice," Vazna states.

"I guess I fucking have."

Vazna clenches his fist and I drop to my knees.

How is he doing this to me? I've been walking around assuming I was more powerful than this. It's quite... humbling. Also, quite humiliating.

"It's the wrong choice, boy," he says. "I have the authority to keep you here to convince you to do the right thing."

"Authority of whom?" I sneer. "The only one you need to ask permission from is my sister and Hell would freeze over before she gave it to you."

"She is free to attempt to rescue you, but she knows the consequences of walking the Earth. Our side will take it as an active attempt to start the Apocalypse and respond accordingly. I am sure I do not need to tell you that we are far more prepared to act on this course than she is. We have had millennia, she has had, what? Six months?" His patronizing tone fires up my protective side.

"You underestimate her," I snarl. "Trust me. If you keep me here, she will go to *any* lengths to get me back."

"Would she? Only she has the power to rescue you and she knows the consequences of coming here."

I blink and look around. We are back on Earth, on top of the mountain.

The penny drops. "You want her to come here, don't you? You want her to start Armageddon."

"It's not our first choice, but like I said, we have waited around for this for a long, long time."

"So rather out of the way and then you can reboot and start again?" I scoff.

"It is merely killing two birds with one stone. You will destroy the box, or we will leave Annabelle with no choice but to start Armageddon to rescue you. The barriers between Heaven and Hell and the Earth will fall away, along with any magick cast and Lucifer will rise up out of that box and do what he always wanted to do. He will run riot over this land and claim it as his own, along with everyone in it including you, including *her*. So, as you can see, you are left with one choice. To destroy the box."

"Fuck you," I drawl. "You can keep me here, but Belle won't start your war for you. You are barking up the wrong Dark Angel if you think she will come here looking for me." A pain in my head makes me pause and take a breath.

"Shax, don't be alarmed, it's Sid."

"Who?" I ask in my head, trying not to grimace in pain.

A pause. "The Night Mare," he clips out.

"Oh," I growl. "You. What are you doing in my head?"

Vazna is giving me an odd look as I hold this private conversation but fuck him. He can think what he likes about me now. He – *they* – have shown me that I belong in Hell.

"Annabelle asked me to seek you out. You need to come back. You need to fix what you broke."

"What? What did I break?"

"Hell," he grunts.

The connection is severed after that cryptic comment, but there is nothing I can do about it. I'm trapped here. The pain of Shadow's banishment blossoms up, causing me to choke.

"Sid?" I venture.

But I know he's gone. I need him to come back so that I can tell Annabelle to stay away and not come to find me.

If she is looking for me because something has happened, though, I fear that she is going to do exactly as the other side wants her to and then we will all lose.

CHAPTER 12

Annabelle

"HOW DO I FIX THIS?" I mutter, staring at Aleister, my hands still gripped in his t-shirt. He is still breathing but it is shallow, and his color has drained so that he is turning gray. "Fix it, Annabelle, fix it."

"How? How?" I suddenly shriek as no one says anything. They are all looking at me, but not helping. "HOW? Dammit! Fuck! Fuck!"

I stand up and spin around, thinking furiously. There has to be a way.

"The Swamp Demons! They are immune!" Shax told me so I know it's true.

Killian is shaking his head. "It's been tried, Princess," he says quietly.

"Fuck!" I scream and spin around again, my hands in my hair.

"Annabelle," Mother's sharp voice echoes through the room. "We were in the middle of a conversation about your brother before you flew out of the room like an Avenging

Dark Angel…" She pauses as she takes in the somber mood. "What's happened here?"

"He's dying!" I spit out. "So, forgive me, *Mother*, if I have bigger things to concentrate on."

"Dying?" she queries and comes further into the room. When she spots Aleister, she pales. "Oh. How?"

"Doesn't matter! I need to fix it. Help me fix it!" I screech at her, completely losing it. I feel like my heart is about to explode into a million pieces and that nothing will be able to repair it. I don't understand this feeling. I don't get it. I don't fucking like it. I want it to end. I want this fucking nightmare to end.

"Baby girl," Mother says calmly, taking my hands. "Breathe."

"I can't," I say, my breath hitching and tears welling up again. My vision goes blurry as the blood pools and then spills down my cheeks. "Now you see why I don't cry!" I shriek, knowing I must look an absolute mess.

"He means a lot to you," Mother says quietly.

I nod. "I can't lose him, Mom. I—I can't…"

"Did you try giving him your blood?" she asks.

I shake my head, but pull away from her, already slashing my wrist wide open with my sharp nails. I open his mouth and pour some inside, then as an idea hits, I also pour some on his wound. He stirs slightly and the nasty hole in his side starts to close.

I gasp and drop to my knees. "Aleister!" My wounded heart starts to heal, but then it shatters all over again as the hole reopens and his head lolls to the side. "No!" I scream. "Aleister, please. Come back to me."

I drop my head to the bed as Mother comes over and places her hand on my back. I can almost feel the glare she is giving the other males over the top of my head, but I don't want them. They can't help. I need someone who can help.

I stand up, shaking her off me. I storm out of the room, the wind whipping around me as I march down the corridor. I hold my hands out and blow doors off their hinges as I seek the someone who can tell Aleister to hang on until I can fix him.

"Annabelle?" Sid asks, poking his head out of a room a few doors down from the destruction I'm causing.

"Sid!" I exclaim and race towards him.

"Annabelle, I have something to tell you…"

"It can wait. I need you to go into Aleister's subconscious and tell him that I will find a way to fix it. He just needs to hang on."

"But…"

"Go, please," I say, trying not to snap at him. My fists are clenched so that I don't grab him and forcibly take him to Aleister.

"Of course," he murmurs and follows me back down the hall.

I enter the room where my Gargoyle is lying on the bed, now turning to stone. I swallow loudly and point to him. "Tell him I will find a way."

I don't even wait for Sid to enter him. I just leave. I can't be here. I can't deal with this type of *emotion*. It's the worst of the worst. I wouldn't wish this on anyone. I was getting used to the more positive emotions, of feeling something other than pleasure caused by the pain of others and my own. I have to think. My brain is clouded. Looking down at Aleister dying is fucking with my ability to think clearly.

I flame outside into the snow and shiver. I breathe in deeply and close my eyes.

"Annabelle?"

I spin around at the quiet voice. "Xavier. I can't talk right now."

She approaches me, dressed in a white silk suit that

makes her look even more the ice princess, especially against this uncharacteristic backdrop.

"You blew the door of the room I was in clean off. Sure you don't want to talk about it?" she asks with a small smirk.

I shake my head. "I don't have time. I need to think."

"About what?"

"A way to save Aleister!" I shout at her.

"Because you love him?" she asks.

I glare at her. Love? What is that even? Is it love if I feel like dying instead of him? Is it love if I want him to open his eyes and smile at me so badly, I feel sick?

"I need him," I state. "He gives a part of me what I want."

"What's that then?" she asks.

I hiss. "I don't have time for this!"

"Humor me."

I let out an exasperated breath. Every second I'm speaking to her, I'm not thinking about a way to save Aleister.

My shoulders slump. "He makes me feel like a *woman*. Not the Queen, not a Demon, not a 'female', just a…"

"Girl in love?" Xavier prompts me.

I clear my throat. "Something like that," I mumble.

"I get that," she says, reaching out to brush my wild, tangled hair away from my blood-stained face.

"Xavier, please…" I close my eyes as I implore her. I don't have time for this.

"Shh," she murmurs.

She traces her cool fingers over my cheeks.

"Relax," she whispers.

I sigh and feel my shoulders lose a bit of their tension.

"I know how you feel," she says, keeping up that quiet, soothing tone as she strokes me. "I feel that way around you."

My eyes fly open. She is standing close to me, her ice-blue eyes hot with desire.

"You're only pursuing me because I'm Queen," I accuse her.

She shakes her head. "Maybe to start. I mean, who doesn't want to be with you? You are Queen, you are gorgeous, sexy, feisty, fierce. I came here intending to make an alliance, but when I touched you the first time, I felt something."

"They all say that," I protest weakly. She is getting to me. She is making me lose my focus. Aleister needs me. I shouldn't be out here allowing her to flirt with me.

But I don't move. Something deep inside me is screaming at me to stay where I am.

She smiles sadly. "No, this is different. You'll notice that my touch is cold. I am that way all throughout my body. My blood is like ice in my veins. I don't know what it is to be warm. Or rather, I didn't. When I touched you, I felt something that I haven't felt, ever. Thousands of years of being frozen, one touch of your skin started to thaw me out. I'm not walking away from that no matter what you say or do to me. You make me feel something, Annabelle. A *real* something. It runs deep. It makes me feel like..."

"A girl in love?" I whisper.

She smiles slowly. "Exactly."

I breathe in through my nose. "I like your cool touch. I run flaming hot. It's a pleasure to have your hands on me."

"Wait until my icy tongue is thrusting up your cunt," she giggles.

"Ooh," I moan. "Stop, I need to think."

"Did you try your blood?" she asks, taking her hands off me and getting down to business.

"Yes. It half-worked, it was like something was missing."

She purses her lips at me.

I stare at them as a thought descends down onto me suddenly and it takes my breath away. "Missing. It is like something is missing. Because something *is* missing!" I expostulate.

She raises an eyebrow at me. "Oh?"

"My blood isn't just mine, like his isn't just his! Shax!" I bellow in her face, gripping her shoulders. "We are twins. We are two halves of the same circle."

"You think mixing his blood with yours is the key?"

"Yes! You did it, Xavier. You calmed me down enough to think clearly."

"You did all the work," she says with a laugh. "And call me Xavi, please."

I return her laugh, knowing that I've got this right. "Come we need to get Shax…" My high crashes so far south, I stumble, my breath whooshing out of my lungs rapidly. I go light-headed. Shax isn't here. He abandoned me, betrayed me and because of that Aleister is going to die.

"Annabelle?" Xavi asks, concerned as I stop dead in my tracks.

"Shax isn't here," I mutter under my breath. "He can't help me."

She blinks and leans forward. "I've heard the rumors about the bat…that it's coated with Shax's blood. Maybe you can use…"

"That's it!" I yell. "His blood. I don't need him. He left me some!" I hold my hand out. The vial full of Shax's blood that I took from his room, appears on my palm from the safe keeping of the, well, safe in my bedroom where I'd stashed it.

Xavi looks at it and steps back slightly.

I grin at her and clutch it tightly. "Let's go."

I *know* this is going to work. It has to. My blood wasn't enough but both of ours *will* work. Gripping her hand tightly, I flame us back into the bedroom where Killian and Elijah are still standing vigil over Aleister, right where I left them. Mom is pacing fretfully.

"Belle, this…you need to say good…"

"No!" I roar at her and disentangle myself from Xavi.

A white mist floats out of Aleister and Sid appears, looking anxious. *More* anxious than usual due to all of the people surrounding him.

"Uhm," he starts. "He is…"

"I'm here," I say, ignoring him. I drop to my knees and talk directly to Aleister.

"Seconds…" Sid mutters.

It gets my ass into gear. I open Aleister's mouth and dump the contents of the vial into it. I slash open my wrist again to make sure he gets a good mouthful of my blood before I shut his mouth, keeping my hand on his chin and hoping he swallows it. He coughs and splutters, so I let his chin go and wait.

We all wait.

There is complete silence.

"Please," I mutter. "This has to work. Please."

I watch as his eyelids flutter and then pop open, looking around at everyone looming over him.

"It worked?" I ask hopefully.

He wipes his mouth with a moue of distaste. I don't take offense as Gargoyles don't drink blood as a rule. Plus, Shax's is probably burning him inside, but mine must be trying to counteract it. I didn't even think about the fact that Shax's blood hurts my Demons. Combined with mine, it heals them. His skin is losing the stony exterior. That's all that matters.

"It worked," he says with a groan and looks at the hole in his side that is now closing and staying closed. "You don't know how close that was."

His slate gray eyes find mine and fill with love. "Thank you," he murmurs.

I kiss him and climb onto the bed. I straddle him carefully. "Am I hurting you?" I ask as I lay down with my head on his chest anyway.

"No, stay right where you are." He turns his head to the side and says, "Thanks for sticking around. It wasn't so lonely."

I glance up to see that he has directed his words to Sid.

I choke back the sob. "I'm so sorry," I whisper. "I'm so sorry I wasn't quicker."

Aleister looks back at me and then his eyes close wearily. He wraps his arm loosely around me. "Your timing was perfect," he says and then his breathing deepens as he falls asleep. I can hear his heart beating strong in his chest and I sigh. I find Sid's eyes and whisper, "Thank you."

He nods and then dissipates, the stress of so many people around him getting to him. I feel terrible. He wanted to talk to me, and I ordered him to help Aleister. I want to follow him, but I don't want to leave Aleister again. Not yet.

The words that I have been too terrified to say to any of them are hovering on my lips, but I just can't do it. Not even now. If I say them and I lose him, I won't be able to go on. I shove them aside and vow never to utter those three words to any of them.

I just…can't.

CHAPTER 13

Elijah

AFTER AXELLE LEAVES, Killian and I move away from Aleister now that he seems to be okay. That was really close. I honestly thought he was a goner.

Annabelle has curled up on him and is holding hands with Xavier, who has moved into a chair to sit next to them.

"Do you think Annabelle is okay?" I ask Killian quietly.

"She will be. She has come close to losing someone permanently. That has never happened before. She's realized that we aren't all as immortal as she is, but she will rise up from that disappointment."

"I hope so. I didn't like seeing her so upset."

"Because you love her," Killian states.

"Do you?" I ask him back.

He ignores me.

The females are talking quietly and then they laugh, looking over at us.

I narrow my eyes at them.

"I'm not sure I like this," I sulk to Lian.

"Ha," he scoffs. "Try stopping it. It's like a freight train on a collision course with an F-15."

I give him a puzzled look. "Huh?"

He shakes his head. "Never mind. Just know that Annabelle is the F15." He snorts at his own joke.

"Whatever," I grumble. "This doesn't bother you?"

His white eyes fix on mine. "Of course it bothers me. You know what will happen if we spend too long together."

I grunt. Hell freezing over will be the least of our worries.

"I don't get it, though," he mutters, glaring at the two females.

"What?" I ask.

"We are not supposed to cross paths. Sure, it's happened once or twice over the centuries, but we are never supposed to be in Hell at the same time. Why is she here? Why was she recalled at the same time I was?" He gives me a perturbed look.

I lower my voice even more. "You think this isn't a coincidence?"

He shakes his head. "It feels deliberate somehow. I don't know… I have to go."

"Where?"

"To Roberta. She is responsible for all of the Demons duties. If she is behind this, I want to know why."

I nod grimly.

He leans forward with a soft smirk. "She's in the room."

"So she is," I reply and meet his lips halfway.

He kisses me gently, sweeping his tongue over mine until I'm ready for more.

He pulls away and murmurs, "I want more time with you, E. Make it happen."

I nod again and wave him off as he disappears in a flash of lightning.

I notice the silence before I see the females looking at me.

"What?" I ask gruffly.

Xavier looks back at Annabelle. "You let them have that?"

"It was part of the deal," she answers with a sassy smile at me.

"Can't wait to see more," Xavier murmurs.

Annabelle looks at her in surprise.

"Just because I don't want one of them to stick their dick in *me*, doesn't mean I don't want to watch them stick it in someone else," she laughs.

"You're perfect," Annabelle snorts with amusement.

If I weren't the Master of Hellhounds, I would probably be blushing right now. No, I definitely do not like this dynamic. The two of them giggling in corners and being all female, probably discussing the size of all of our dicks.

"Humph," I mutter and then step forward. "I have to go."

Annabelle is climbing off Aleister as if I'd lit a fire under her ass. "What?" she snaps. "Are you fucking joking?"

"Nope. I wasn't finished with my duties when we found the Gargoyle outside. I have to go back and finish up."

"Not a fucking chance, puppy," she snarls at me. "You think I want to go through this again? You are not moving out of my sight."

"You let Killian go," I point out, secretly pleased she is being so protective, but needing to maintain a nonchalant air.

"Ugh, he's different," she spits out.

I can't tell if she is pissed off or turned on by that fact.

"I'm going," I say. "You forget that I am at least three times the size of Darius in my natural form."

She gives me a raking once-over with those wicked green eyes. "Mm," she murmurs. "Yes, you are."

"So, I'll see you later," I say and bend down to kiss her.

"If you aren't back in ten minutes, I'm coming to find you, so be quick about your business," she says, turning her head petulantly so that I catch her cheek instead of her lips.

"Yes, Ma'am," I drawl with a mock salute and whirl out of the room before she can change her mind.

Not that I wouldn't mind her accompanying me, but I don't want the distraction. I really do need to finish feeding the Hounds. They will be livid by now.

As I land in the kennels, I know I'm right. They are snarling and growling at each other. I quickly go about appeasing them and five minutes later I stretch. I'm itching to Shift.

I undress quickly and fling my clothes in a pile on the floor. I drop to my knees and let it wash over me. I feel my bones stretch and break, making me grunt. My back arches and snaps, only to reform again. My head Shifts to the middle head of the Hound and I grow an extra two, one on either side.

I let out a low rumble, snapping my strong jaw, feeling my teeth sharpen and my hands and feet turn to massive paws.

As the Shift finishes, I shake out my fur and rip out a loud howl to let my Hounds know their true Master is here.

I pad around the kennel, feeling at ease in this skin. I turn in a circle and decide to take a nap, forgetting all about Annabelle's warning. I don't sleep much in my human form. I crashed earlier in Anna's bed after all the sex for a few minutes, but during a Shift is when I get most of my sleep. Unlike the recycled Demons, I need a bit of sleep now and again.

I'm about to curl up when her scent fills the air.

I sniff wildly as she appears in the kennels, flames surrounding her. "I told you ten minutes, you prick," she hisses and then pauses as she sees me in my natural form, towering over her. "I see," she adds.

I gaze at her, waiting for her to move.

She doesn't.

She stays completely still.

It makes the predator in me start to pace around her, sizing her up.

"Trying to intimidate me, puppy?" she asks gently.

I snort, enjoying this immensely. She isn't scared but she is cautious. I could still eat her whole. I pause to wonder what would happen to me if I did. Would she burst out of me, killing me in the process, or burn her way out of me, also ending my life? Either way, I'll be dead.

I shove my big middle head in her face and lick her.

She turns her head to the side.

I've grazed her cheek raw with my rough tongue. I want to apologize, but the beast is salivating at the smell of her blood. I pant heavily, ruffling her hair away from her face.

I lower my head further taking in her stretchy black vest top and black jeans.

"What are you thinking?" she murmurs to me.

I let out a grunt. She doesn't want to know what I'm thinking. It's dark and filthy.

She reaches out to stroke my right head with her left hand and my left head with her right. My middle head curls my lip up at her.

"Sorry, puppy. I've only got two hands," she giggles. "Show me what you want."

I wish that I could tell her, communicate with her while I'm in this form. But no amount of forcing my thoughts on her tells her what I want.

I reach up a massive paw, hooking one of my razor-sharp claws onto her vest top, pulling down and shredding it completely.

"Oh," she says with understanding, taking a step back from me.

I get a faint whiff of alarm from her but if she was truly scared, she would flame herself out of here away from me, back to the safety of her residence, which I cannot enter in this form.

The seconds tick away as I wait to see what she will do.

CHAPTER 14

Annabelle

I LICK MY LIPS. I know exactly what he wants from me. I figured as soon as I saw him in this form that he would be thinking it. Earlier when we were fucking, he went into a partial Shift. I wouldn't have said 'no' if he had Shifted completely and I'm not going to say no now. I don't know how this will work but I am completely hot for him right now.

He can smell my arousal, I know it.

He ducks his head, wedging his middle nose in between my legs to breathe in deeply. He lets out a low rumble of appreciation.

I take a deep breath, mentally preparing myself for this. I have never engaged in Shifter sex before. Unless you count my experience with Razor in serpent form, which, now that I think about it, I suppose you can.

That was different though. I know Elijah's dick in human

form is a monster cock. Just thinking about his Hellhound appendage is making my palms sweat.

"You want me, puppy?" I murmur. "Like this?"

Of course he doesn't answer me. He can't but his actions tell me all I need to know. He swipes his huge paw, knocking me off my feet. I land on my back with a loud "Oof!"

He is looming over me in the next second, lowering his head to flick his sharp tongue over my exposed nipple.

I arch my back as he scrapes my skin raw but the pleasure it sends to my clit makes me moan.

He moves his head down further and nuzzles the zipper of my jeans. I push on his huge head to get him to move up enough so that I can flick the button undone and wiggle out of them. I want to do this manually, giving both of us the time to think about this thoroughly. There will be no going back from this.

He shuffles back as I strip off, his eyes, all six of them, riveted to my pussy. I toss my jeans to the side and lie back, opening my legs wide for him.

He growls softly, pressing his nose to my pussy again and breathing in. He flicks his tongue out, grazing it over my clit making me yelp with mingled pleasure and pain.

I gasp as his right and left heads push my legs open even wider and then their jaws clamp down on my inner thighs, holding me in place as he thrusts his sandpaper tongue up my cunt.

"Fuck," I scream and writhe on the hard stone floor of the kennels.

We are being watched by all of his Hellhounds. I'm glad they are all restrained in the separate holding pens or I'd probably be eaten alive. As it is, it turns me on even more.

He rumbles loudly as I coat his tongue with my cum.

"That's it, puppy. Tongue fuck me good," I pant, raising my hips up to meet his thrusts head on.

He stops suddenly. He lifts his middle head, letting my legs go as well. I'm panting fiercely, not really ready for this to end. Plus, I haven't gotten my hands on his cock yet.

His evil yellow eyes gaze into mine and then with another swipe of his paw, he flips me over onto my stomach.

I suck in a breath knowing we are really doing this now. He is going to fuck me in his Hellhound form and I'm going to let him.

It makes me so wet, it sets off his sensitive nose. He buries it between my legs again as I get to my hands and knees.

"Fuck me, Elijah," I whisper to him, giving him my consent to do this. I doubt he would stop now even if I told him no, but I also know that he is very aware that if I didn't want this, I would leave. "Split me in two with that Demon cock."

He snarls at my words, pushing my legs further apart with his head. I look over my shoulder and see him looming over me. He is gigantic.

I shiver in anticipation.

"Fuck," I moan. "Take me now, puppy. I need it."

He licks me all the way up my back, scraping my skin off. I see him plant his massive paws on either side of me, just a little way in front of where my head is. I start to shake with nerves. He smells it, so do the other Hounds.

They start to yap uncontrollably as he mounts me as best he can with me being so small underneath him.

I push my ass out and open up as wide as I can. I feel his tip pushing against me but there is no way he can enter me. My cunt hole just isn't big enough.

He grunts softy and pushes forward, tearing me apart.

I scream as he gets his tip in and keeps shoving.

"Fuck, Elijah," I screech as he rips me.

He does nothing to make it easier on me, if anything he gets even rougher.

He rams his cock into me, splitting me wide open. The blood is gushing down my thighs mingled with my cum as I'm so wet from this filthy fucking. If anyone walked in now, they would get a show that would stay with them forever.

"Yes!" I scream, gritting my teeth, clenching my fists against the floor.

He latches his middle mouth onto the back of my neck to keep me in place. I'm being pushed away from him the deeper he gets into my body.

"Fuck! Fuck!" I scream "Fuck, yes! All the way, puppy, ride me so fucking hard."

He grunts loudly, his right and left heads dripping drool all around me he has finally shoved his entire girth into me. He settles for a moment and then he rides me.

Hard and fast.

I'm breathless with pain and pleasure all mixing together to form the dirtiest erotic moment of my entire life. I don't think there is anything in the sin bin that can top this.

The feel of his colossal cock thrusting deep into me, ripping me, tearing my cunt apart makes me come suddenly and violently. I shudder uncontrollably as I clench around his dick again and again, screaming his name.

"Harder! Harder!" I cry out.

He gives it to me. He fucks me in a frenzied mating that takes my breath away even as I moan loudly, begging for more.

I can feel him hitting my womb, knowing that his whole length isn't inside me.

I want to change positions but there is nowhere for me to go. He has me pinned in place and due to the nature of his animal form, I can't ride him. Not the way I want to anyway.

I slam my hips back onto his cock impaling myself again and again until I climax in a spectacular display, squirting all over the floor underneath me as I lube up his dog's dick with my cunt juice.

"Fucking Hell!" I roar as the orgasm thunders through me, making my clit thud and my pussy walls clutch at him desperately.

He whimpers softly as he lets go of my neck and thrusts one last time, drenching my body with his flood of cum, which spills out of my torn pussy and pours onto the floor on top of my squirt fluid.

I haven't even caught my breath before he Shifts to his human form and takes me in his arms, wrapping them around me tightly as he draws us to the floor gently, away from the puddle.

"Thank you," he murmurs to me. "Oh, thank you, Anna. I'm sorry for hurting you but I knew you could take it. Thank you, baby. You can't know what that felt like for me."

I smile smugly to myself, not giving him an answer that he doesn't require anyway. *He* has no idea what that felt like for *me*.

If he thinks this won't happen again, he is sorely mistaken.

I cuddle into him, giving him the comfort he needs from me, assuring him that I'm okay after the roughest sex I've ever engaged in.

My cunt has already healed, so when I roll us over, I finally get the chance to take him the way *I* want to. I ride him hard, flicking my fingers out to open the cages of the panting Hellhounds.

They descend on us in a pack of fur and fangs as I laugh with delight at how this afternoon has turned out.

CHAPTER 15

Sid

I CURL up on the floor even more if that's possible. "Get out of my head," I mutter to her.

"No can do, baby," Leviathan purrs. *"I am going to haunt you until you get me the fuck out of here."*

"I can't do that. Leave me alone."

"Nope. I am staying right here. I'm bored and you are so easy to wind up."

"Please," I whimper, clutching at my head.

"Oh, baby. You can't get rid of me. You are made from me. We are one and the same."

"I am nothing like you. I never was," I whisper.

"Keep telling yourself that, lover. Also, this whole wounded bird thing you've got going on with Annabelle is a treat. She is falling for it hook, line and sinker. This can work to my advantage."

"Go away," I moan. She is making my head ache with her incessant babbling. This has been going on since I left Razor's body and the safety of the fire cube. She has latched onto me and she won't let me go. "What do you want from me?" I ask her desperately.

"I want you to convince Annabelle to set me free, obviously," she scoffs.

"She won't. I can't help you."

"Convince her or I will be here tormenting you until the end of time. Every time you look at her knowing how insecure you feel about her, I will be here to remind you how worthless you are. She will never love you, Sid. You are a hideous monster. You tortured her in her sleep. Do you really think that she can ever love you? She is using you, you pathetic little freak."

I whimper as everything she says, I know is true. "Please," I whisper. "Please stop it. She cares about me."

"Aww, baby. You are so deluded. She doesn't care about you, only what you can do for her. Look at the other men she is with! Do you think you can compare to them? Live up to the hot alpha males she fucks at every opportunity? What do you think she is going to do when you bed her? You will fall woefully short and she will leave you because you'll have served your purpose and the pity fuck she owes you will be over with."

"No! She doesn't pity me. She doesn't!" I try to convince myself that Annabelle isn't like that, but the doubts, they are there, they are real and having Leviathan scream my weaknesses at me every second of every day will only make them stronger.

"Pathetic and deluded."

"Shut. Up," I grit out and turn over on the floor, but no amount of fidgeting will get her out of my head.

"You know how," she replies in a steady voice.

There's a knock at the door. "Sid?"

I sit up and look over the bed at the door. "Annabelle?" I mutter.

"Sid?" The door opens a crack. "Are you in here?"

"Yes," I say quietly. I'm hurt by the way she treated me

earlier. I understand her urgency, but I had something to tell her and she brushed me off.

"May I come in?" she asks, poking her head around the door.

"Okay," I say, staying where I am on the floor, with the bed in between us.

"That's pity on her face."

"I'm sorry for earlier," Annabelle says, biting her lip. "I was distraught, frantic and I felt helpless. I needed a minute to think clearly and I knew you could tell Aleister to hold on while I found a fix. I shouldn't have talked to you the way I did. I owe you everything for what you did for Aleister, and I was a horrible bitch."

I blink at her and stand up. "I understand," I start.

"You're a fucking pushover. A weak pushover."

I grit my teeth. I can't listen to her. I can't.

"It's okay," I add as Annabelle gives me an odd look at my hesitancy.

"Are you sure?" she presses.

I nod.

"What did you have to tell me?" she asks, coming closer.

"It's about Shax," I say. "I went to him."

"What?" she asks, her eyes going wide. "But that would've hurt you. You didn't have to do that."

I shrug as Leviathan laughs and laughs in my head.

"Are you buying this? Really? She couldn't care less about your pain."

"It's okay," I mutter. "He is being held captive by the other side. I don't know many details, but I got that much."

"WHAT?" Annabelle thunders but then presses her lips together.

I know that I flinched at her temper and she reined it in. That proves to me she cares about me.

"You are worthless, Sid. Remember that. Worthless and weak."

I try to fight back the tears that are threatening to come out.

She's right. I am worthless and weak and disgusting.

"I'm sorry," Annabelle says. "I'm just...they're holding him against his will?"

I nod because I can't speak.

We stare at each other for a moment and then she steps into my personal space. I want to shrink back but she wraps her arms around me.

"You repulse her," Leviathan comments. "I can feel it radiating off her."

"Do I repulse you?" I blurt out, hating myself even more for sounding as pathetic as Leviathan tells me I am.

Annabelle pulls away from me with a horrified look on her face. "No!" she exclaims. "Absolutely not. Sid, where is this coming from?" She strokes my mangled face, searching my eyes.

"Your males are pretty to look at. I am not. I don't understand what you see when you look at me." The courage that it took to say those words has worn me out. I feel like collapsing at her feet and never getting back up.

"I see you," she says gently.

"She's talking around it, lover. She is clever with her words."

I frown at Annabelle. "What does that mean?"

"It means that when I look at you, I see your essence, Sid. You are a beautiful being. Do you want me to show you how I feel about you?"

"Oh, please," Leviathan scoffs.

"H-how?"

"I want to have sex with you. I want to take you in my arms, kiss you, make you feel safe and secure as we take pleasure in each other. I want to show you that I don't care about your exterior."

I don't answer her. I can't. The thought of having sex with her terrifies me. I can't open myself up to her, not like that.

Devlin's words echo in my head, but I still can't bring myself to say 'yes'.

"You aren't ready yet and that's fine. I *am*," she says. "I will wait until you are ready too and then we can show each other how we feel."

"Are you seriously buying this?" Leviathan asks. "She is using you. You have a talent that she needs."

"Stop it!" I spit out, pushing Annabelle away from me and clutching my head again. "Just stop it!"

"I'm sorry," Annabelle whispers, wringing her hands. "I didn't mean to scare you."

"No, it's not you…"

"Sid. Do you not believe that I care about you?"

"I'm worthless and weak," I mutter.

"No!" she says adamantly, taking my hands away from my head and kissing them. "You are beautiful and strong, and I care about you more than I can actually say. The words… they are difficult for me. Actions? Now that I can do. Tell me what to do to prove to you that I want you."

"Tell her to release me, Sid, or I will be here every time you talk to her, think about her and if you do finally fuck, I will be in your head telling you how awful you are and that she is faking every second of being with you."

I shake my head.

Annabelle sighs and I know that she is losing patience with me. She drags me closer to her, pressing her lips to mine, kissing me fervently until I open my mouth and let her tongue touch mine. I moan as the happiness I feel from this one kiss is overwhelming.

She wraps her arms around me, squashing her body against mine.

I freeze.

I could do this when I was inhabiting Gregory's body. It was easy. Now I am more afraid than I have ever been. What if I disappoint her? What if I don't please her? What if she compares me to the bigger, badder Demons and I fall woefully short?

"You won't please her."

Woefully short. Those are Leviathan's words, but they ring true. I can't please Annabelle.

It hurts my heart more than I can handle, but I put my hands up and push her away from me.

"Sid," she says. full of sorrow.

"I will try to contact Shax again, find out more, but please go now," I croak out.

She hesitates, but then she nods slowly. "Okay. But please, Sid. You have to trust me."

I give her a blank look as I'm struggling to stay on my feet now.

"I will prove myself to you," she says getting mad.

She is beautiful with her eyes flashing.

"I wouldn't do this for *anyone* else. I don't chase, Sid, but you? You *are* fucking worth it and I will make you see that."

She storms out of the room, slamming the door behind her.

I smile.

She is fierce and I love her. I just wish that I could show her or tell her.

I know that I can't do that with Leviathan casting doubt and poking at my insecurities all of the time.

"That's right, baby. Come to me."

I dissipate and rematerialize next to the cell she was shoved back into.

"I can't get you out of there," I say. "Annabelle's magick is too strong."

"But?"

"I will find a way to get her to release you, okay? But you have to leave me alone. I can't think with you in my head all the damn time."

"Aww, it's sooo much fun fucking with you, lover."

"Get out of my head and I will get Annabelle to let you out."

"Sorry, but that doesn't work for me. How do I know you will keep your end of the bargain?"

I grit my teeth. "Give me a few days, please. I need you out of my head to think."

"Three days and then all bets are off. If I'm not out of here in three days, Sid, I will come back to torment you so badly, you will find a way to kill yourself and end your misery once and for all. Are we clear?"

I swallow back the pain of her words and make a deal with the creature who wishes she was the Devil but falls *woefully short*. "Yes. We have a deal."

CHAPTER 16

Drescal

I'VE FINALLY TRACKED Anna down to the main gallery. "There you are," I say, leaning casually in the archway. I don't want her to think that I've spent the last ten minutes frantically searching for her.

"Hey," she says, glancing briefly at me before she goes back to looking at the huge painting of her parents.

I cross over to her and wrap my arms around her, nuzzling her neck.

She sighs and leans back into me.

"It's a magnificent piece," I comment.

"It is. I miss him so much."

"I know you do, baby. You'll get him back."

"The other side has Shax. They're holding him."

I frown at her words. "Oh?"

"Yeah. Assholes. I have to go and get him back."

"Of course you do. We will help in any way that we can. How did you find out?"

"Sid has been to Shax. It hurts him to go, but he went anyway."

She sounds sad. She is very protective over the Night Mare. Lucky fucker, indeed.

"You and him? You're a thing now?" I ask as innocently as I can for a Demon with nothing but her on my mind.

"Not really. He won't…he *can't*… Where have you been?" she suddenly snaps at me, pulling away to face me. "I needed you, *all* of you and three of you were nowhere in sight."

"Ah, yes." I'd figured this would come back to crush my nuts. "We heard about Aleister and we're sorry that we weren't there for you. We were…"

"What?" she snarls as I stop speaking, trying to find a way to tell her without making her even more venomous.

"He wanted to talk about options," I say with a sigh.

"Who? What?" She shakes her head, confused.

"Gregory. He wanted to talk about his options," I say with a sigh. "He wanted to talk to Dev, I tagged along to add in my two cents, you know?"

"Oh," she says surprised. "Why didn't he talk to me about it?"

She is upset and I hate that I caused that and will hurt her further. "He didn't want to. He wanted a guy's perspective, I guess."

"I see," she growls.

Gregory is going to be in for it when she catches up with him.

"What did you advise him?" she questions as I knew she would.

"That's up to him to tell you, not me, Princess."

"Knew you'd say that," she grouses, but then smiles. At least I am off the hook. "Thank you for helping him."

"Anything for you," I murmur and cup her face.

I bend down to kiss her, lapping up her deliciousness, and

pushing her back against the wall underneath her parent's portrait.

She giggles and looks up. "I'm dirty, but not that dirty," she snorts.

I smile at her. "I need you," I murmur. "Ever since Killian branded you, I'm feeling a bit…lost."

"What?" she asks with a frown. "Don't be ridiculous. It doesn't mean anything. It was tit for tat, that's all."

I glare darkly at her. "That brings me to the brand that *you* gave *him*."

She returns my glare. "Do you want me to brand *you*?" she asks.

"Yes," I murmur to her surprise. "I want the whole of Hell to know that I belong to you."

"Oh!" she moans, closing her eyes in bliss. "You are perfect, you know that."

I grin to myself. I knew that she would cream herself over that. I'd known as soon as I saw what she did to Killian that I'd ask her, and I also know the others won't be far behind with this thought. Seems I got to her first, as I'd hoped.

"Perfect for you," I mutter.

"That you are. You make my blood tingle," she purrs.

I give her a surprised look. "I do?"

She giggles again, looking down shyly. It's fucking adorable. "Yeah, you always have. It's why I kept you around. You and me…we're connected somehow."

"*That's* why you kept me around?" I ask, put out. "I thought it was because I got you off like no other?"

"That too," she laughs at my insecurity. "My body responds to you."

"I love you," I blurt out. "I don't expect you to say it back, but I need you to know every day how I feel about you."

A cloud passes over her face. "That brings me to something that I need to say."

"If it's about Xavier, then I am way ahead of you."

We lock eyes for a brief moment before she says stiffly, "Go on."

I sigh. "I know that your intention is to bring her into our circle. I need you to know that I won't be affected by her."

"Meaning?" she growls at me.

I glare at her. "You know what I am, Anna. You must've thought about it."

"I have," she says quietly. "I don't feel that I have much to be concerned about, but that is more down to her than you."

"Ouch," I growl back at her. "That's not fair, Anna."

"I know, but I can't help that."

"I told you that I will never be with another female again and that remains the truth. Whether Xavi is here or not doesn't change that. At all. I love you. You have always been the one, Anna. Another female here won't affect me, I can assure you. I have absolutely no interest in her and I never will."

Silence.

Then she grins at me. "I know. I was only messing. I trust you, Dres."

Bitch. She was testing me.

I laugh. "You are infuriating."

"I know. Look, I know that having Xavi here is unexpected. I know that having only males here will be easier for you, but that's not how it's panned out. She gives me a big part of what I want. She is staying, just so that is absolutely clear. If you did ever develop feelings for her, and don't insult me by denying that you might. Forever is a long time, Dres. I'm being practical. *If* you ever did develop feelings for her. Tell me the second you suspect, please. That's all I ask. I'm pretty sure that she will never touch any of you, but I want to know about you. Okay?"

I grimace at her. "I agree that I will tell you if the Incubus in me requires more. We have already had this discussion. However, I will point out – again – that other females don't do it for me anymore. I will expand on that to stress that they don't affect me *at all*." I give her this ass backwards information and hope that she doesn't make me say it in actual words.

She presses her lips together as she takes that in and then she struggles not to laugh in my face.

"Are you being serious?" she snickers.

I grit my teeth. "Yes," I spit out. "Are you happy now? Secure in the knowledge that I won't fuck around?"

"Quite!" she exclaims and laughs so loudly, I feel like disappearing into the floor.

"You are a bitch, you know that, finding my affliction so hilarious."

"I'm s-sorry," she splutters. "I just…I just…oh, the devil's horns. You are precious, my sweet Incubus."

"Thanks," I growl.

She grabs my duster tightly and drags me towards her, kissing me fervently, her hands going to my dick. I'm glad to note that I've got a raging hard-on just from her kisses.

"Just checking," she smirks, giving me a squeeze.

"You don't need to worry about that," I say. "I just want to fuck you all day, every day."

"Wouldn't that be nice," she sighs, going melancholy. "Maybe one day when things aren't quite so…chilly."

"I'll hold you to that," I whisper to her. "Go and do what you need to, Princess. I will catch up with you later."

She nods and with a last lingering kiss, she flames out.

Feeling a bit more secure in my relationship with Anna, I decide to head off to speak to Devlin. In spite of Annabelle's words of trust, she is going to need to hear from each of her males in turn about their loyalty to her. I know that none of them would ever fuck around on her. I've been observing, taking in every second of their interactions with her and they are as besotted with her as I am. Having Xavi here isn't going to change that, but she needs to know.

Before I go, I look up at the portrait of Luc and Axelle and give the former Devil a quick salute. "Thanks, old friend. You pulled me out of that particular fire with your daughter. I owe you."

CHAPTER 17

Annabelle

I FIND XAVIER in the sin bin, twirling around a stripper pole slowly even though there's no music.

I watch her for a minute before she knows I'm there. She is graceful and beautiful. I click my fingers and a soft, sensual beat pulsates out of the speakers, echoing around the empty room.

"Hey," she says, stopping and looking over at me.

"Don't stop. I just put the music on," I tell her, moving closer.

She giggles and wraps a long leg around the pole and dips back. Her light blonde hair is a cascade of gorgeousness that makes me lick my lips.

She straightens up and lets go of the pole. "You want to talk?"

"Yeah," I say, folding my arms across my chest. "Just a few things we need to get straight."

"What's that then?"

"What I expect from you."

"One-way street?"

"You'll get your say."

"Okay," she says, also folding her arms, "What do you expect from me?"

"Friendship," I say, surprising her.

"Oh?" she asks, a disappointed look falling over her lovely features.

"I have never had a female friend before. Well, in actual fact, I have never had a friend before. Not a real one. Not even Shax really. There are things that I can't talk to him about. I feel comfortable around you. I feel like we are similar in the way we think, and I know that I can talk to you about anything. That said, I'm also very attracted to you."

"So, a friend with benefits?" she asks.

"If you want to look at it that way," I reply. "I want to pursue a sexual relationship with you, but first and foremost, I want you to be my friend."

I gulp as I realize how desperate that sounds.

She smiles at me. "I want that as well," she says softly. "I, too, have never had a friend, female or otherwise. When I was sitting with you earlier and we were talking and holding hands. It was…" She sighs happily. "It was what I've been searching for my entire existence."

"So, we are clear?" I ask.

"Friends first," she says with a bob of her head.

I smile at her. "Good. Now that we've cleared that up, I do need to tell you that we can't pursue the sex side until I've spoken with all of my males in turn."

She narrows her eyes at me. "You answer to them?" she asks with a small laugh.

"No. But the fact that you have a pussy and will be around during my sex with them is something that needs to be addressed before we go ahead."

"Will they be around during your sex with me?" she asks carefully.

"What are your thoughts on that?"

"Hey, I don't mind being watched. But like I've said, I don't do dick."

"They won't lay a finger on you. They will draw back a stump if they touch you."

"Is that for *my* benefit or yours?"

"Mine," I say, trying to remain calm. "You're a big enough badass to look after yourself. They won't touch you because they are here for me. I don't doubt any of them. I just want to make it clear that I'm taking you at your word."

"You should. I have no ill intentions. I know that actions speak louder than words and all that. I will prove to you that I am only interested in you. What the males do isn't my concern. If they want to fuck your ass, while I lick your cunt, then good for them. I'm here for you, well, and me, obviously."

Her words reassure me. I wasn't overly bothered. I trust my males. But she is an unknown and one that I need to get my ducks in a row with. The lines have to be clear because there can be no blurring of them. I just won't allow it. "Glad that is sorted because it would really piss me off, on an already shit day, to have to throw you out of here."

She snickers. "Phew," she says, pretending to wipe off her brow.

I giggle. "You got anything to add?"

"Nope, we are on the same page, Belle. Can I call you Belle?

"Only Shax calls me Belle," I tell her, feeling that particular pain hit me in the chest.

"So that's a no?"

"No, it's a yes."

She nods. "Belle, then. I can honestly say that the idea of

being with a male is as off putting to me as being with a Swamp Demon. You have nothing to worry about from me."

"Or me," Killian's voice says from behind me. "We've already talked about this, Princess. However, I feel under the circumstances, a reiteration is required."

"I definitely wouldn't do *him*," Xavi says with a loud guffaw.

"Hey!" I exclaim. "*I* do him."

"And how I pity you," she says with a sassy smile, which makes me laugh.

I turn to Killian. "Tell me again."

"Only your pussy, Princess, and I don't do anal with females. So, now that we've cleared that up, there is something else more pertinent that we need to discuss."

I feel the dread well up in me. It's a horrible feeling and one that I'm not used to, but this day just seems to be going from bad to worse.

"What is it?" I ask with a sigh.

He walks in between me and Xavi and then to the side a bit so that we are standing at the point of a triangle.

"I don't know how much you know about the Horsemen," he starts.

"Enough," I say warily.

"So, you know that once you walk the Earth, the four of us will be called to you, the Anti-Christ, to start the Apocalypse?"

I nod.

"I begin with War, then comes Pestilence, Famine follows and finally Death."

"Okay," I say. "I know all of this. Get to the part where it's all doom and gloom."

He gives me a filthy look which makes me smile.

He walks over to Xavi, his hand held up. She looks at me

and then holds her hand up. When their hands touch, the ground beneath our feet starts to shake.

"What the fuck?" I ask, grabbing onto the nearest chair to keep myself steady.

They pull their hands apart.

"We are not meant to be near each other until the time comes," Killian says. "There has been a fuck-up in Admin. Xavi wasn't meant to be recalled so early, while I was still here."

"Why?" I ask with a fierce frown that gives me a headache.

Killian's white eyes find mine. "Roberta is denying all knowledge of it. I don't know if she is behind this or not, but someone is. Someone wanted two of us here together."

"What for?" I ask perplexed. "It's not like we can start the Apocalypse from here."

The look he gives me tells me that I am dead wrong with that thought process.

"What?" I ask. "We can?"

"The four of us are here for you," he says. "We converge at your behest. If we are on Earth, this will be automatic, but here in Hell...we could destroy it if all four of us are called back here at the same time. We will start the Apocalypse, but it will be here."

I close my eyes as I take that in.

"Are you fucking kidding me?" I hiss.

"I wish that I was, Anna, but sadly, Xavi and I being here together is dangerous for us all."

"So, are you asking me to make a choice? To send one of you back?" I thunder at him. "Not happening, War. You are mine, both of you. Fuck the Apocalypse. Neither of you are going anywhere."

"That is, of course, your call," he states. "I am merely giving you the facts. The omens have already fallen and will continue to fall while we remain here together. If Famine or Death arrives…"

"Stop!" I say, putting up my hand. "If Roberta knows about this now, she will make sure they don't come here. I do not believe that she is the mastermind behind wanting to destroy Hell. Why would she? She runs this place more than I do."

"I tend to agree, but who can really know for sure?" he asks.

I pause as something he said sinks in. "What do you mean the omens have already fallen?"

"The snow," he says. "I think it occurred because Xavi arrived here while I was still in residence."

"No," I say, shaking my head. "That happened because Shax left."

"Perhaps. Perhaps not," he says mildly.

I pinch the bridge of my nose. "Fuck's sake," I mutter. "Anything else?" I yell at both of them. "Do either of you have any more bad news to give me? Anyone? Any-fucking-one?" I scream into the empty sin bin turning in a circle.

As my luck would currently have it, a creature steps out of the shadows, a dead Griffin flung over his shoulder. "Actually, Ma'am. I do."

"FUUUUUUUCCCCCKKKKKK!" My roar echoes around the residence, bringing one and all to me. I kick the chair that I'm next to, sending it flying off and nearly smacking Killian in the head on its way to the other side of the room. "Fuckity-fuck-fuck-fuck!" I snarl as the creature comes closer. "Start talking."

CHAPTER 18

Shax

I TAKE A DEEP BREATH. Sid has just left my head again after I told him to tell Annabelle to stay away. I have a plan that will get myself out of this disaster, for which I have only myself to thank. Perhaps, also Luc. If Belle does open that box, I will kill him for real for doing this to me.

"Asshole," I mutter.

I watch Vazna closely. He is talking in hushed tones to two more Angels that have shown up and are just as arrogant and irritating as Vazna is. I know that I don't want to be associated with them. The 'Angel' part of me goes very firmly hand-in-hand with the 'Dark' part. I accept who I am, and it is like a weight has lifted off my shoulders. The sorrow of what happened to Shadow settles back down though and until I can get back to Hell and find out for sure what happened to her, I can't think about it much. It hurts and I don't want to hurt anymore.

"I'll destroy the box," I call out during a pause in their conversation.

Vazna hesitates in turning around to face me.

"I'll destroy the box, but you let me go back to my sister," I add, just so that the deal laid out is clear.

"What changed your mind?" Vazna asks.

I sigh. "Look, I don't really give a shit one way or the other. Annabelle hasn't arrived to save me so that kind of tells me all I need to know about *her* loyalty," I drawl, hoping that I sound convincing. "It's not my fight. I just want to go back to Hell, find Shadow and live my life."

"The female has swayed your decision," he states knowingly. "I knew that using her would make you see sense. Very good, Shax. We have a deal."

The clap of thunder and strike of lightning does nothing to soothe my unease about how simple that was.

I gulp, hoping that I have the capacity to execute this stupid plan. I have never suffered from inferiority before. Not even with Annabelle. I always knew that she was better than me, stronger, faster, huge destiny and all that. I've never wanted any of that. The thought of her responsibility, that her life isn't really her own, makes me shudder and pity her. Okay, well, not *pity* her, she would kill me on the spot if she thought that, but it's close. I certainly don't want to be her.

Vazna approaches me slowly. He scrutinizes my face, probably to see if he can see any signs of deception. It's not difficult for me to keep a bland expression on my face. I think it's my natural reaction to anything. He must decide that he can trust me as he waves his hand and releases me from the cage he put me in. Either that or he is waiting for me to run.

I don't run.

Running would be foolish.

I walk steadily forward, my eyes on the box that is just hovering there on a cloud, all innocent and shit. If anyone came across it, they wouldn't think anything of it. They wouldn't know that the end of the world resides in it. They wouldn't know that this Pandora's Box needs to get back to Hell and that I will take it there or die trying.

Die trying.

I guess that is a strong possibility.

"So, do I just bleed on it?" I ask, as I really have no clue.

Vazna frowns at me. He doesn't know either. "Perhaps, along with an *inferno* spell?" he suggests with a moue of distaste.

"Sure thing," I mutter, but have absolutely no intention of doing it. I have to grab this box, sprout my wings and fly off this mountain before the three Angels can tag me.

Easy fucking peasey.

I reach out, my hands shake slightly which pisses me off.

"Slowly," Vazna murmurs as if the thing might detonate at the slightest vibration.

I suddenly realize that he can't touch it. It doesn't come as a big surprise though. This thing is completely evil. There isn't a shred of good in it or about it. I lick my lips and place my hands either side of the box, still not touching it.

I decide that it's now or fucking never to get this shit done, when I'm suddenly blown backwards from the box by a flash of magick that hurts my eyes.

"You!" Vazna hisses.

I can feel the power as he draws out his sword of light and it burns my retinas so that I can't see at all. I put my hand up to my face, the sheer terror that Annabelle has fucked off what I said and come anyway, ricocheting through my body.

"Belle?" I cry out.

"Go!" my dad roars at me, shocking me to my core.

"What the fuck?" I yell back. "What are you doing here?" I don't expect an answer and I don't get one. I can't see fuck all except flashes of blinding light.

I scramble backwards and get to my feet. Then I lurch

forward, hands stretched out, feeling for the box. My hands land on it at the same time that one of Vazna's Angel friends grabs me and yanks me backwards.

"Gah," I choke out as his hold on my t-shirt strangles me.

But the box is in my hands.

Well, not quite *in* my hands but hovering next to them. I can see the blurry shape of it in front of me. It has latched onto me, my power, and it gives me all the strength I need to kick back, catching the Angel in his knee. I turn and with my right hand – the left still reached out for the box – I blast him with a bit of Dark Angel magick that sends him flying off the mountaintop. Vazna might be one thing, but these plain old garden variety Angel dicks are a whole other ball game. I look over to see my dad, black-feathered wings out, battling with Vazna, swords clashing and magick flying all over.

"Go!" Dad shouts at me. "Get that fucking box back to Hell – now!"

"Got it," I mutter. There is absolutely *no* defying him. He was Hell's Guardian during Luc's reign, after he fell from being *Heaven's* Guardian. Normally pretty laid back, he has gone into feral protective mode and I pity the poor asshole who is standing between me leaving this mountaintop and him.

I would stop to help him, but this box is currently not leaving the vicinity of my hands. Every time I move them, Pandora's Box, as I've come to think of it now, moves with them. I can't fight, I can't throw magick that will be very effective with one hand. So, I stash my pride, grip the box now with my bare hands, hissing as it scorches the skin off my palms and sprout my wings.

"See you at home," I yell and take off, swooping past the other Angel who is trying desperately to get away from my father's wrath and Vazna, snarling like a stabbed Hellhound.

"It's been a riot," I mutter and then I'm gone.

I land in the Wastelands, my hands on fire, but safe with Pandora's Box as I walk through the gates of Hell. I'm home.

CHAPTER 19

Gregory

"Uʜᴍ," I mutter as I step forward to calm Annabelle down. No one else has moved a muscle, so I'm guessing this has fallen quite definitively into *my* camp. Fair enough. I am currently treating her for anger management. I have come across plenty of unstable characters in my time, some down-right dangerous. Granted, they are no Anti-Christ, but still. I know how to handle myself around an angry creature.

"Annabelle," I say calmly, but loud enough for her to hear me.

"Not now, Gregory. Counting isn't going to cut it."

"I get that, but perhaps consider taking a deep breath and closing your eyes for a moment. When you open them, see that you have your circle around you. You don't want to hurt them. They are here to help you."

Her furious eyes land on mine, but to my surprise, and everyone's relief, she does as I say.

When her eyes open again, she grimaces at me. I think it's meant to be a smile, so I return it.

She turns to the creature with the dead something slung over his shoulder. It looks like a Griffin but who really knows?

"Who are you?" she barks out, but with a little less bite than before.

"Franklin, Your Majesty. I work for Darius. We found this…" He dumps the Griffin-creature on the floor, "… outside your residence."

"Did *you* kill her?" Annabelle asks.

Franklin shakes his head. "Nope. Found her this way."

Annabelle edges closer to the dead creature, staring at her. She bends down slightly and gasps. "Shadow?" she murmurs.

"You know her?" Franklin asks.

"She's my brother's pet!" she snarls. "If I find out you had anything to do with this…"

Franklin holds his hands up. "No, Ma'am. We found her this way."

"Dammit," she mutters and strokes the Griffin's head.

A morbid silence falls, but then we all jump backwards, Annabelle included as the Griffin Shifts into a human-looking girl with a loud moan.

"Fucking Hell!" Annabelle exclaims. "You Shift?"

"Shax!" Shadow cries out, scrambling naked to her feet. "Is he…?" She doesn't wait for an answer, she just runs head-long out of the sin bin, into the night, with the Demon Guard hot on her heels, yelling at her to come back.

"Wow," Annabelle says. "I did not know that the Griffins Shifted."

"They don't," Killian states. "They also don't come back to life. You are oddly connected to that creature."

"It must be through Shax," she mutters, but then shakes her head, fixing him with a vicious glare. "Stay away from Xavi until I can think about this. Xavi, you stay away from

Killian. This is *not* an invitation to fuck off. Yes, War, I'm talking to you. You stay put. I will figure this out."

Killian nods grimly and stalks off back into the residence. The only other female in the place, who I'm going to assume is Xavi, nods primly and then twines herself around a stripper pole as the rest of us look away.

"We need to talk," Annabelle says to me, grabbing me by my hand and leading me away before she flames us out, back to my chosen bedroom.

"Holy shit!" I exclaim as the feeling of being on fire, but not, mangles my brain cells. I clamp my lips shut as she gives me a death stare. "*Un*holy shit?" I mutter a moment later and it elicits the smile I was hoping for.

"Better," she says with a smirk. "Thanks for that. I don't know what it is about you, but you know the right thing to say to stop me from…" She makes an explosive gesture with her hands.

"Do you need to talk?" I ask. "We haven't had a session for a couple of days."

"Yes, please," she breathes out and sits on the edge of the bed. She doesn't wait for me to settle; she just launches into everything that's on her mind. Xavier – who I now know is the Horseman of Pestilence; why the two Horseman being together is bad news; her fear over nearly losing Aleister; Shax's betrayal and finally her frustration at me.

"That's not fair," I tell her when she accuses me of not going to her about my options. I knew Drescal would tell her what we talked about.

"You want to know about options for staying here with me, you talk *to me*," she grits out.

"I understand your annoyance that I went to Devlin and not you. But something he said to me this morning stuck with me. I figured he was the one that would give it to me straight, but also not try and eat my head off at the same time."

She giggles in spite of her exasperation. "Yeah, don't mess with Elijah when he's in his natural form. He will break you in two." She gets a dark look on her face as she pauses but then she smiles. "So, what did you decide upon?"

"Nothing," I say truthfully. "I don't…"

"Say no more," she says, holding her hand up. "It's a big decision. But that's why I wanted to be a part of it. I want you to be informed and know your options." She stands up and crosses over to me, sitting in a big armchair. She surprises me by crawling into my lap.

She settles comfortably and places her head on my chest.

I have practically stopped breathing. I don't want to move in case she disappears. Letting out a sigh, she puts one hand on my waist, the other next to her head.

"I don't want to lose you, Gregory. I can make you like Devlin, you could live forever, but as yourself."

I was expecting it. Devlin told me as much that this was going to be her plan. He didn't sugarcoat it though. The process is painful, frightening and then there is the whole control over the dead aspect, which will take some getting used to.

"I know," I say, "and it's an option."

"Please don't take too long to decide," she whispers. "After nearly losing Aleister, I don't want you any more vulnerable than you have to be."

"Okay," I say and kiss the top of her head.

She looks up at me with those mesmerizing eyes and I can't help myself. I fall forward into a kiss with her that is so breathtaking, I go lightheaded. She rises up, cupping my face, pressing her body closer to mine, gyrating over the painful bulge in my pants.

"Fuck me," she rasps against my lips. "Please, Gregory, I need to be that close to you. I can't wait any longer."

I moan into her mouth. I can't wait either. I'd wanted to take her this morning, but she rejected me.

"What's changed?" I ask carefully, not wanting her to stop rubbing herself over my cock but needing to know.

"You are serious about staying here. Devlin spoke to you about becoming a Necromancer and you didn't run a mile in the opposite direction."

I chuckle. "No, I didn't run. I want to be with you, Annabelle and I have a choice of how to be. I guess seeing as I'm going to be stuck with that choice for eternity, it has to be the *right* choice, you know?"

"I know," she says and then kisses me again, swirling her tongue against mine in a hypnotic rhythm that I fall into completely.

She rips the buttons off my shirt, then pulls her vest top over her head to expose those magnificent breasts to me which I've been fantasizing about since I got here.

"Oh, yes," I murmur, rubbing my thumbs over their peaks and then dropping my hands to her tiny waist. "You are gorgeous."

"Mm," she purrs and slides my zipper down, slipping her hand into my pants.

Her light touch grazes over my rock-hard cock…

"Shax!" she bellows suddenly in my ear, making me crash down from the high I was flying, in the worst way possible.

"Uhm," I mutter, horrified and completely in shock that she called out her twin brother's name while we were making love. "Uhm…" I stammer again as she climbs off me and drags her top back on.

"He's home!" she cries out and lunges for the door, yanking it open and coming face-to-face with her twin. "You fucker!" she roars at him blasting him back from the doorway with magick. I stand and zip up my pants, bewildered by what is happening here. At least I can rest assured she wasn't fantasizing about her brother while she was with me. She merely felt his presence on the other side of the door.

I can't help but mutter, "Thank fuck for that," as I watch the two fight it out with a large wooden box in between them, that I'm guessing houses Annabelle's father and...I gulp...Lucifer.

CHAPTER 20

Annabelle

I AM FURIOUS! I'm trying my best to batter the fuck out of my twin as we wrestle on the floor, regardless of the impact it will have on my own face, but this fucking box won't get out of his way. It's like it's protecting him or something.

Panting, I sit back and punch him in the nuts, feeling the sharp pain in my own crotch but I grimace and ignore it.

"You fucker!" I shriek at him as he groans and curls up into a ball. "You absolute traitor!"

"Not a traitor, you bitch," he rasps. "Here's the damn box."

I blink and look at the box.

"You're fucking welcome," he grouses and sits up. "Hope that hurt you as much as it did me."

I press my lips together to stop the laugh. I launch myself at him, box be damned and hug him from the side tightly.

"I missed you, you dick. Don't ever leave me again. You can't…the implications…"

"I'm not going anywhere," he reassures me, giving me a swift kiss on my forehead.

I frown at the box. "You can put that down now. It's hurting you."

He glowers at it. "It's burning my fucking hands off, but I can't get rid of it."

"Get Axelle," Killian's calm voice comes from over the top of my head.

I don't know who he spoke to but when I look up, it was Gregory. He rushes off and I feel bad. Then I groan and feel terrible.

We were about to get it on with some serious sexy time and not only did I put a stop to it, I called out Shax's name while I had Gregory's dick in my hand. What must he think?

I put my hand to my face and take a breath, shaking it off.

"Start at the beginning," I say to Shax.

He stands up and I stand with him, putting my hands over his. I can control the pain, the Hellfire, it is mine, but Shax's hands are destroyed.

"Give it to me."

"I can't," he says. "I wish I could, but it has attached itself to me."

"Oh?" I ask curiously and stare intently at it. I try to take it off him, but I can't.

"Shax!" Mom calls out, appearing next to us and staring at the box before she goes around it to hug him. "Is that it?"

He nods grimly. "But without a doubt, Lucifer is inside it as well. Vazna wanted me to destroy it. He says only my blood can either destroy it or open it."

"What?" I ask in confusion. "What about the key?" I bring the key that Elijah kept from me to my hand and insert it into the lock.

"Annabelle!" Mom snaps at me, clutching at her throat.

I turn the key, ignoring her and everyone else's protests but nothing happens.

"Told you," Shax says with a sigh. "There's more. This was

Luc's plan all along. He made sure that Vazna ended up with the box and that Vazna found me. It was his plan that I destroy the box with them all inside."

Mom strangled gasp is barely audible over my own. "Liar," I hiss. "Dad would never have said that. That Angel prick lied to you."

Shax shakes his head. "There was a letter from Luc. I know it was from him, there was something personal between us. He knew I would question it and made sure that I knew it was his wish."

"No," Mom chokes out. "Luc wouldn't do this to me."

"I'm sorry, Mom," Shax says quietly.

"Damn you," she hisses at the box and places her hands on it. It releases Shax from his hold on it and hovers in the air between them.

"Well? What the fuck are you waiting for? Open the damn thing!" I bark at him.

"No!" Mom says, putting her hand up. "If we know for definite now that Lucifer is inside it as well, we have to think about this. Be ready." She waves her hand over it and the box disappears.

"Mom!" I growl at her. "What the fuck are you doing? Don't you want Dad back?"

"Of course, I do," she hisses at me. "But there are things about Lucifer that you don't know," she adds icily.

"Oh, I know," I snarl. "Dad told me all about how you are supposed to be Lucifer's Demon Bound to breed the fucker that he wants to take *my* place." I jab my thumb in my chest.

My mother's blue eyes bore into mine in fury. "He had no right," she says stiffly. "But you see how this affects me as well as all of my children. You aren't ready to take him on, Annabelle. He will kill you and Shax and this baby that I'm carrying and then rape me until he gets what he wants."

Out of the corner of my eye, I see my males all take a

giant step back from us. I don't blame them. That was harsh and makes me feel like shit for more than one reason. "You don't think I can beat him," I state coldly.

"He is so much older, more…"

"If you say more powerful then you are dead wrong," I snarl. "The power of Hell is in me. I *know* what I can do. None of you have seen the tip of the iceberg, so *do not* tell me that he is more powerful than me because he isn't. The power is mine now, not his."

"We can't rule out that he still has every ounce of that power. He never died. Your grandfather imprisoned him with his full power still available to him. Consider that the power of Hell didn't so much transfer as expanded to include the new ruler in his absence."

"Bring the box back," I grit out.

"No, not until we have a definitive plan. One where I *know* you can beat him."

"Dad will help me, if I need it," I point out triumphantly, having landed on this suddenly.

"Not a solid enough plan if Lucifer gets to you first," she says stubbornly.

The frustration wells up in me and I clench my fists.

"Where is Dad?" Shax asks suddenly in the dark silence that has fallen. "He should be back by now."

"Back from where?" I ask.

"He was the one that rescued me," Shax says with a frown.

"Yes, your little mind-fuck friend came to me after he spoke with Shax," Mom says, surprising me completely. "It was a trap for you to start the Apocalypse. You couldn't go, so Dashel went to get his son back from those assholes."

"Sid?" I ask, feeling the betrayal. "He came to see *you* instead of me?"

"Mm," she says. "Killian, be a dear and go and check on my husband, would you?"

"Uhm," I interject before Killian can respond. "You don't order him about."

"It wasn't an order," Killian says and feels the wrath of my gaze as it lands upon him. "She asked and, yes, I'll go."

He steps forward to kiss the top of my head. "I'll be right back."

"No…"

"It will give Hell a chance to adapt to having only Xavi here, if only for a few moments," he whispers to me, lifting my chin up. "Trust me, Princess. I will return shortly. I won't leave you, no matter how dire this situation gets."

"If you aren't back in five minutes, I will come to find you and fuck Armageddon, got it?"

"Got it," he says with a soft smile that I have never seen cross his face before. I find it a massive turn on that he has that side to him. I grip his shirt and tilt my head back expecting a proper kiss even though my mother and brother are standing right here.

He obliges me briefly and then with a bolt of lightning that singes the carpet in the hallway, he's gone.

"He had better come back," I spit out at my mother.

"They can't touch the Horsemen," she says, with a wave of her hand. "They are inevitable."

"Humph," I mutter. I look at Shax. He looks completely beaten. "I'm glad you're back and safe."

"Thanks," he mutters. "Have you seen Shadow?"

I frown at him. "Yeah, the Guards found her dead outside and brought her to me."

"Dead?" he croaks out.

"Oh, she's fine now," I add, probably belatedly. Maybe, I should have led with that. His face went a sickly color of gray and the penny drops. "You knew she could Shift into a human, didn't you?" I ask.

"She's fine?" he asks, ignoring my question.

I nod. "She was dead, but when I touched her, she came back, then she ran off back outside. I dunno how or why. Shax?"

But he is off down the corridor before I can stop him.

I flame out and appear in front of him. "You can't go out there. With the lockdown and the climate change, Darius is on the rampage for offenders. You go out there, he might tag you. He already nearly killed Aleister. I can't let you leave here." I put my hand on his chest to make my point.

"I'll be fine," he dismisses my concern. "I need to find Shadow."

"Nooo, you need to stay here where you are safe." My eyes bore into his. He has to realize that if he gets hurt so do I now that he is back. Yes, our blood might be the cure to the briar poison, but what if he dies before he gets back to me?

"I'm going," he states and shoves me out of the way.

"Shax!" I call after him, but he has vanished in a flurry of black feathered wings.

I'm about to follow him when I suddenly just lose all the fight that's in me.

"Fuck this," I comment and flame out.

I land in my bedroom. I'm tired and the weight of Hell on my shoulders has never felt so heavy.

"Hey," Xavi says, startling me. She is sitting on my bed, her legs crossed, wearing an ice blue silk wraparound dress that has fallen away to show off her thigh.

"Hey," I reply.

"Thought you might need a friend," she says. "That sounded kind of intense."

"Guess you're up to speed on the Hell-family secrets, huh?"

She shrugs. "I'm not interested in spilling sordid tales, if that is concerning you."

"I didn't think you would."

"Want to talk about it?"

"Not really?"

"What to fuck then?"

"Now you're getting warmer," I reply with a laugh.

She gives me a slow smile and stands up, arms at her sides, legs slightly apart. She wants me to unwrap her and not even the rampant Hounds of Hell could stop me.

CHAPTER 21

Annabelle

I REACH out and pluck at the small bow just above her hip that is keeping her dress closed. I tug on it gently and step closer as her dress falls apart, not enough to expose her body to me, but enough to entice.

I flick the fabric away from her, dragging it down so that it drops to the floor in a silken pool.

My eyes take her in hungrily. She is beautiful. I've fucked females before, but only for fun. There were no feelings involved one way or the other. This is new and exciting. It makes my heart beat that bit faster.

She reaches out to the hem of my vest top and pulls it up and over my head. I hear her breath catch. "Get on the bed," she murmurs.

I do as she asks, crawling into the middle and then turning around.

"Lie down," she instructs.

I do, flicking the zipper on my jeans undone.

She gives me a soft giggle and pulls my jeans off me to dump on the floor.

Her eyes go wide as she takes in the branded 'K' on my mound. "Oh," she breathes out, tentatively touching it with her cool fingers. She traces the shape of it, her eyes hooded. "He really loves you," she murmurs.

I want to ask her how she knows that about him, but I don't. Instead, I brush it aside with a scoff. "It's possession, nothing more."

Her eyes shoot up to mine. "No," she says, shaking her head. "He wouldn't do this."

Now, I can't resist. "How do you know so much about him?" I ask.

She laughs gently. "We were close once, and no, not in that sense. When Lucifer created us, we had our purpose, but no catalyst. Once he found his Demon Bound, we had to scatter as we had no idea if his child would be the Anti-Christ or not, and so on and so forth."

"I understand," I say. She seems sad, wistful.

"My touch can kill a being if I choose it. It took centuries before I could control it properly, I damaged everything that I touched. It broke something in me, I think. Something that I never recovered from. But he listened to me when I talked and he understood, I think."

"Friends," I murmur.

"Perhaps," she says, losing the sadness as quickly as it came. "It may have been many centuries since we spent any time together, but I don't think he has changed. At all. Except with you. His expression lightens when he looks at you, he has made you his."

"I also made him *mine*," I point out. "He did this in retaliation."

"I don't believe that. That's petty and War doesn't do things that are insignificant."

"You know him better than I do, I find that troubling," I say, sitting up and leaning on my elbows.

"Don't read into it, Belle. You've known him for five minutes. He and I were made from Lucifer's blood at the very beginning."

Is it me or does that *not* make it any better? Still, she has a point.

Letting it go, I flop back to the bed and open my legs in invitation.

She giggles again and then dips her finger into my pussy, giving me a gentle finger fuck before she withdraws it to rub over my clit.

"Mm," I sigh as it feels so good. The ice on her fingertips is cooling my anger.

She ducks her head and I gasp as her tongue flicks my clit. She pushes two fingers into me again and crooks her fingers, finding my G-spot instantly.

"Fuck," I cry out, arching my back as she manipulates an orgasm out of me in seconds.

She looks up from tongue fucking my clit and grins. "Bet not even the Incubus can do that."

"Nope!" I pant. "Fuck."

She withdraws her fingers and replaces them with her tongue. She thrusts it up into my hot cunt and the sizzle is unmistakable. Steam rises from the combination of her cold touching my hot.

I laugh in delight and so does she.

"Oh, that is classic," I snort. "More, more!" I wiggle my ass on the black silk sheets to get closer to her mouth again.

She lowers her mouth to me and uses her tongue and fingers to make an orgasm fire through me that I won't forget in a hurry.

Panting, I watch as she rises up over me, licking her lips.

"Delicious," she purrs. "Taste."

She kisses me, slipping her tongue between my lips. I kiss her back, devouring her mouth as I rake my sharp nails down her back. Her hand goes into my hair, twisting it and pulling so that I moan into her mouth. Then, she leaves my lips to close her mouth over one of my nipples. She pinches the other one and twists it roughly before dropping her fingers back to my pussy.

"Yes," I sigh, bucking underneath her.

"Are you pleased with me, my Queen?" she murmurs, eyes lowered seductively.

"Oh, yes," I sigh happily. "Very pleased. I want to repay the favor."

"No," she says, shaking her head. "Not this time. I want to watch you take pleasure from your males now."

Xavi sits back and I see that they are in the room with us. Minus Killian, which concerns me briefly, and Gregory. I make a mental note to go and speak to him about what happened earlier. But first, I want to be fucked every which way, in every hole that I have by the males assembled before me.

Xavi climbs off the bed and drapes herself on the chaise, eyes on me. She doesn't even glance at Devlin, who is the first to strip off and join me. I tear my eyes away from hers and fixate on Devlin's baby-blues.

"Tell me what you want," I whisper to him. "Use this body to fulfil your fantasies."

His eyes deepen to a navy blue that takes my breath away. "What I want from you is too dark, love," he whispers back.

"Try me," I say, gripping his shoulders and drawing him closer to me.

He settles in between my legs and I wrap them around him. I whisper in his ear so that the others can't hear me.

"What I want from you is black and filthy," I murmur.

He turns his head slightly, his eyes narrowed. "Oh?"

I turn his head again so that I can speak to him and him alone, whispering the dirt into his ear.

"I can Astral out of my body, Dev. The body is me, but without powers. I want you to take that body and hurt me. I want to feel the spike of fear and I want to run. I want you to chase me down and when you catch me, I want you to hurt me some more. I want you to humiliate me, degrade me completely. I want you to force me to service you. I want you to take complete advantage of me. Can you do that, baby?"

He has stopped breathing. He has frozen in place.

Slowly, he turns his head to me, his eyes questioning. When he sees that I'm being deadly serious, he lowers his mouth to my ear. "Rapeplay?"

"You got a problem with that?"

He breathes in deeply through his nose. "You are soo bad, love."

He hasn't answered me which disappoints me. I figured he would be the one after he wanted me held down last time.

He pushes down on my hips and slides into my wet pussy with a look of bliss on his face. "We'll talk about it more," he finally says and then pounds me into the bed.

I grin up at him and roll us over. "Dres?"

He is already there. He sticks his fingers into my full pussy and wiggles them a little bit. When they are wet enough, he withdraws them and lubes up my ass.

He guides his cock into me as Devlin continues to thrust into my pussy.

I close my eyes and revel in the hedonism of the moment.

When I open my eyes, I glance at Xavi. Her fingers are coaxing an orgasm from her clit as she watches me get fucked in both ends.

As our eyes lock, she comes, shuddering on the chaise as it sweeps over her in wave after wave of ecstasy.

"Keep going," she pants. "You can handle more than that."

I grin at Elijah. He is naked and jerking off to make his dick as hard as he can for me to take in my mouth. He pushes it through my lips as Aleister joins us on the bed.

"You okay?" I ask around Elijah's engorged cock.

He nods, his eyes dark.

I take him in my hand and make him rock-hard. I alternate my mouth and hands between him and Elijah as Devlin and Drescal pound my holes until I scream with the intensity of the climax that thunders over me.

"More!" I cry out. Drescal makes room for Elijah behind me and I let out a loud groan as I feel him pushing at my asshole, stuffing his monster cock inside me alongside Drescal's huge dick.

"Fuck, yes," I breathe. "All of you."

They get my meaning and it's too much for Devlin, who has been fucking me the longest. He spurts his load into me, his cum flooding inside me and mingling with my own.

"Fuck, love," he rasps. "Get her on her feet," he adds to the others.

Dicks are withdrawn and I'm hauled off the bed.

I catch my breath as Xavi sits up, her eyes now riveted to this show.

Drescal and Elijah stand behind me and lift me up off my feet. Devlin and Aleister grab my ankles as Drescal and Elijah find their way back into my ass in this position. I groan as they bury themselves deep into me. Devlin and Aleister push my legs straight up into the air and move in closer. I rest my ankles on their shoulders as they guide their cocks into my pussy together.

"Oh, unholy fuck!" I roar as all four dicks pound me at once.

I am completely impaled on cock. I can't move a muscle in this position. Luckily, I'm a flexible bitch and also a fucking dirty one. I'm loving every single second of this gangbang. The only thing that could make it better is if Killian were to arrive and give that dark look as he calls me his filthy whore. I want it. I need it. I'm craving the degradation so badly, I whimper.

"Killian!" I bellow as I just can't take it anymore. "Where the fuck are you?"

I come then, clenching around Devlin and Aleister, coating their cocks with my juice.

Then, I feel him there. He appears next to us with a curious look on his face as he takes in the situation. His hand reaches out and closes around my throat. He squeezes a lot harder than I expected him to.

I nearly choke as he whispers, "That cunt is mine. Who gave you permission to get it fucked like a little slut?"

As I'm jostled about by the force of four Demons screwing me, I grab his hand that is wrapped around my neck and give him a vicious smirk.

"You think this is dirty, War? You have no idea how many dicks I can take."

"Spoken like a true whore," he drawls disinterestedly and releases his hold on me. To the males, he adds, "Use her body until the four of you are completely worn out. I want her like a rag doll before I fuck her until she begs me for mercy."

Xavi hisses. She is standing up and her hands are glittering as they are hooked into claws. "You are going to let him talk to you that way?" she snarls.

"Yeah," I pant as Drescal thrusts up high into me before he comes with a loud grunt. "I'm his disgusting skank and I love it!"

Her eyes flash with understanding and she sits back down as I laugh maniacally.

Drescal has pulled out of my ass and is now attempting to get his cock in my pussy, wedged between Devlin and Aleister.

"That's it, baby. Stretch me, tear me wide open," I scream.

Elijah's hold tightens on me, growling loudly in my ear. He bruises my hips as he grunts loudly, unloading into my ass. He drags me off the other males and throws me on the bed.

"Give us a creampie, Queenie," he pants.

I snort with delight and turn around giving them what they are all slobbering over me for.

I call out to Xavi as they descend on me, dicks, fingers and tongues ravaging me.

She climbs on the bed and crawls over to me. I flick my Devil's serpent's tongue at her and she moans, settling herself over my face so that I can lick her clit.

Who knows what happens after that? It's a tangle of limbs, a cacophony of desire, lust in its rawest form until my body is used one last time to make them come. Then, I'm handed over to Killian, limp, sweating, bleeding from several orifices and barely conscious.

He cradles me in his arms as he croons words to me that make me shiver. "That cunt needs to give my cock a thousand strokes, dirty whore, then you can rest."

CHAPTER 22

Killian

I LOOK DOWN at the Demon Queen, limp in my arms and smile benevolently at her after my words. She is completely worn out but there is no way she will admit it to me. She will do as I ask.

I carry her to the bed and drop her lightly onto it. She groans and flops back, but it makes me laugh gently when she lifts her knees and opens her legs.

I lean over and grab her hips, flipping her over.

"On your knees, bitch. I want to fuck you like an animal," I growl at her.

She lets out a strangled moan and catches Elijah's eye. He is at her side in an instant, letting me know that something that I'd hoped I would see, has already happened. I grip her hips tightly in protest and haul her up to her knees on the edge of the bed and then push her forward slightly. She slumps forward, resting her cheek on the covers. Seeing her like that, with her ass stuck up makes me rethink my whole stance on female anal. Her rear hole is gaping from the double penetration and is very enticing.

"Can't say I'll be that active, War, but have at it. This pussy is yours to do with as you will."

"Dangerous words, Princess," I murmur as I drop my pants.

Elijah strips off the rest of my clothes. I am already rock-hard. It was difficult to stay out of the orgy before. I have never seen a female used so brutally before and still ask for more. She is, without a doubt, the perfect match for me.

Elijah's hand brushes over my cock and it catches Annabelle's attention. She twists her head even more to look at him touching me.

"You don't get off that easily," I say to her, stroking her behind and batting Elijah's hand away.

Then I grab her hips and ram my cock straight into her hot, soaking wet pussy. She is so lubed up with cum, she is slippery, and it takes all my focus not to slide out of her as I pound into her.

"I say you give up and come way before a thousand strokes, mate," Devlin says, laying down on the bed next to Annabelle and playing with her hair.

She snorts in amusement but doesn't say anything.

"Bets?" he adds.

I grunt at him and ignore the other assholes as they take him up on it.

Annabelle winces with each stroke as I steadily pound into her. I have my doubt about this now as well. She is too wet. She is making it too tantalizing for me. My dick is soaked. I can see the cum on it as I pull out only to thrust back inside her. My balls are already aching to release into her, but I have to keep going. A hundred strokes aren't enough.

Devlin is watching intently. I know he is counting. I roll

my eyes at him as I grab Annabelle's hips and redouble my efforts to focus. But all I can think about is adding my cum to the mix that is already inside her. It is arousing me more than I could have possibly thought.

With a soft grunt, I pull out of her and flip her back over. I grab her ankles and drag her down the bed, sliding back into her without missing a beat.

"Damn," Devlin mutters, his eyes going a darker shade of blue that I find quite mesmerizing in the heat of the moment.

"War," Annabelle complains, wiggling on the bed. "I'm fucking raw."

"Oh no, sweetheart, you are as wet as I've ever felt you. You can take this."

"Fuck," she screams as Elijah must take pity on her or some bullshit and leans over to lick her clit, soothing her as I abuse her. "Fuck!" She comes quickly, but it is nowhere near up to her usual level of orgasmic ability. Even so, I've never felt a pussy clench so tightly around my dick before.

"That's it, dirty skank, milk me hard," I pant lightly.

"Fuck, Killian!" she screams and bucks wildly.

Hearing my name on her lips, swollen from being kissed and bitten, I know I'm close to losing it. It is impossible to hold on to my climax with her. I just can't do it. Her nipples are like bullets and even though Devlin is sucking on one of them gently, I know he is still counting.

I don't give a shit. I'm going to have to unload into her any second now. My ego can take the hit because they know what it's like to fuck her.

"Oh, War!" Annabelle screams as I thrust even harder into her, ready to release.

She comes again, this time with a lot more force than before. Her body convulses as her cunt clutches my cock in a death grip.

"Fuck. I fucking love you," I growl and that's it. I can't

stop the flood that explodes out of me and into her.

"What?" she bleats, sweating and still panting as her climax isn't done yet. "What did you just say?"

I grin at her. "I fucking love you, Princess." I thrust one last time and I'm drained.

Devlin looks up from sucking her nipple and states, "Number of the beast, baby. Six hundred and sixty-six strokes. Why does that not surprise me in the least?"

"Fuck," Annabelle laughs nervously as I withdraw from her, still as hard as when I entered her. "Fuck." She scrambles off the bed and rushes to the bathroom. "Fuck!"

I give the slammed bathroom door a curious look.

"I'll go," Xavi says, rising from the chaise where she'd been watching this with disinterest.

"No. I'll go," I say, intrigued by her reaction.

I stalk over and shove the door open.

Annabelle is staring at herself in the mirror. Her eyes meet mine and she grimaces at me. "You couldn't wait to say that until I looked prettier? I'm a fucking mess." She runs her hands through her sweaty tangled hair.

"If I'd waited, it wouldn't have meant as much," I say, wrapping my arms around her. I don't know what it is, but I want to hold her, keep her safe. *Protect* her. Even though she is the ultimate power, she looks so vulnerable right now.

"You're an ass," she says. "You don't even mean it."

I narrow my eyes at her. "Don't I? You know my feelings better than I do now?"

"I can't say it back to you," she blurts out. "So, I hope you weren't expecting it."

"Not at all. I've made my feelings perfectly clear."

"Yeah," she says and pulls away from me. "I need a shower."

"Of course," I say, slightly bewildered by her sudden cold attitude.

"Killian," she says quietly as I turn to leave.

"Yes, Princess?"

"I knew you couldn't get to a thousand," she says, laughter twinkling in her wicked eyes.

I snort. "Not with you," I say and open the door to walk back into the bedroom, closing it quietly behind me.

"Is she okay?" Xavi barks at me the second she sees me.

"Yes, she's having a shower. I think we *all* need to leave her to rest now. She has had a long day and she has shit to deal with tomorrow that is going to take its toll."

Xavi wants to protest, but after I give her a fierce glare, she backs down. "I just want to check on her," she says and stalks past me to the bathroom.

I let her go and turn to the other males. "Next time, E," I say, getting dressed by snapping my fingers.

He nods, disappointed that we didn't get to fuck. I am too, but the rules are the rules it seems, and Annabelle is out. She really does need to rest.

"We will congregate in the Dining Hall first thing tomorrow. I'm going to try and find Shax, make sure that he remains well."

The rest of the males don't give it a second thought, but I saw Annabelle's hands when she was with Shax in the hallway. His were on fire and so were hers. She was controlling it at great cost to her, but I saw it. Somehow, through a bond that I do not understand, they are connected. He hurts, she hurts, and vice versa. However, I feel it is only when they are in Hell together. It's this place. It binds them on a deeper level.

I grit my teeth and speed up my search. I cannot let anything happen to Shax, and therefore Annabelle. Not now. The portents have started, and I think she is very much aware, if not fully informed, by how connected *we* are to each other now.

CHAPTER 23

Annabelle

THE FOLLOWING MORNING, I stare out of my bedroom window at the landscape outside. It's sunny. The snow has disappeared and a bright sun that has *nothing* to do with my illusion power, is shining brightly against a blue sky across the whole of Hell.

I sigh and take the cup of coffee that Xavi hands me. "Is this to do with you?" I accuse her gently.

She laughs. "Shax is back, so probably," she says matter-of-factly.

"Great," I mutter and take a sip.

She puts her arms around me and rests her head on my shoulder. I kiss the top of her head. She stayed with me last night after the orgy that wore me out completely. I have *never* been tested that much in the sack before and I loved it so hard, I want to do it again tonight. It was Killian's words that threw cold water on me. I didn't expect it from him. The others, yeah. I can handle it from them. I *want* it from them, but War? I had set my heart on cool with regard to him. He makes me feel…I can't even describe what I feel when I look at him. It is undeniable, it is electric, it is…inevitable. I don't understand his words of love to me. I didn't think he was capable, and I'd figured he was like me and wouldn't – *couldn't* – say them. I don't know whether to believe him or not. Did he just say them in the heat of the moment? He doesn't seem the type but…

"Still thinking about Killian's declaration?" Xavi interrupts my thoughts.

I snort. "Uh, yeah. I don't think I will get past it soon."

"He means it and he wants you to say it back. Why won't you?" She delivers this query quietly before she hides behind her own mug of coffee.

"I can't," I say and leave it at that as I turn from the window and her. "I need to check in with my mom."

I wave my hand over the wall and a projection appears. We'd spoken last night before I crashed. Dashel is home and safe, having kicked the ass off of Vazna, which is no less than he deserved. Fucker. It seems that War wasn't needed after all.

"Hey," Mom says warily.

I don't blame her. If I'd been at full capacity last night, we would've had a totally different conversation about the box.

"Change your mind yet?" I ask, but with a smile so she knows I'm not ready-to-kill-her-mad. I'm close. She made a decision that she had no right to make. Xavi disagrees and gives me a fierce glare. Apparently, I'm not seeing the bigger picture.

"Nope," Mom says, with a shake of her head. "My babies mean too much to me. I will live without your father if it means keeping you safe."

I gape at her and her bold statement. "You don't mean that," I scoff. She is bluffing. She and my father are destiny.

They will still be as besotted with each other in a million years time. I know it.

She sighs. "I do. I've been up all night talking to Dashel and Evan about this. You will not convince me to give you that box based on your father alone, baby girl. Do better." She cuts off the call to my utmost shock.

"What?" I ask perplexed, turning to Xavi.

She just gives me a told-you-so shrug which I respond to by giving her the finger. "I need to speak to Shax," I mutter, stalking to the bedroom door and yanking it open. I also need to speak to Gregory about our tryst yesterday that got cut short way too soon. Not to mention, I need to find Sid. I'm not angry with him for going to my Mom and Dashel about Shax. It got the job done without any nasty consequences, which is great because I can't deal with any more shit right now. However, we didn't leave things that well between us yesterday, so I *do* need to find him soon.

I walk up to Shax's door, hearing the usual, comforting soft thump of Morbid Angel filtering out of the speakers. I also hear fucking, so I turn tail and head off in the opposite direction, intending to speak to Gregory.

Xavi is close behind me. She has barely left my side since yesterday. She has also taken on a rather submissive role which makes my skin prickle with raw, unadulterated lust. She is one of the most powerful Demons in Hell and yet she wants me to dominate her. It's extremely satisfying on a level that I didn't think needed attention. She is full of surprises and delights.

I'm pulled up short by the massive frame of Roberta suddenly appearing right in front of me.

"Fuck it, bitch. What?" I growl at her, trying to deflect from the fact that she startled me. My rep would take a serious hit if word got out this massive whale of a Demon made me jump.

"Would you mind coming with me?" she asks, giving Xavi a wary look briefly before turning her attention back to me.

"I'm busy. Can it wait?"

"Hmm, I suppose, but I'd rather get it out of the way," she replies.

"Ugh, fine," I grumble and wait for her to disappear first.

Xavi takes my hand and says, "I'll come too, if that's okay?"

"'Course," I mutter and flame us out to Roberta's office, where she is waiting seated behind her huge desk with a stack of files.

I sit in the uncomfortable chair on this side of the desk, Xavi stands behind me with her hand on my shoulder. "Okay, I'm here. What is it?"

She clears her throat. "You've been in power for six months now and your father wanted me to see how you were doing."

"I'm great, thanks," I say and stand up.

"Hang on, Your Majesty, that wasn't an inquiry," Roberta says. "We did an assessment."

"We?" I ask, sitting back down with a fierce frown.

"This office conducted a review on you with all of Hell," she states.

I blink at her.

"Excuse me?" I snarl at her after a beat. "Are you being fucking serious?"

"Quite," she clips out and shoves a stack of the folders at me. "These are the ones that aren't all that enamored with you and your rule, but the top one is the worst by far."

"Oh, really?" I bark at her and snatch the top folder, flicking it open with a death stare at Roberta for this betrayal.

I scan it briefly. It is a load of bullshit in my opinion. She doesn't get this job *at all*. 'I'm too harsh'; 'I don't give enough attention to the newbie Demons'; 'I'm too cold and unapproachable'; 'I'm a big slut'; 'she could do this better'.

The list goes on and on.

"Who wrote this?" I ask, taking a deep breath through my nose.

Roberta smirks at me. "A newbie Seductress Demon," she says, trying not to laugh at the irony of the slutty remark.

"Oh," I say, also trying not to laugh now. "And she thinks this will what? Get my attention? That I'll make her my best friend so I can ask her advice? It's pathetic. Does she have *any* idea how hard this job is? I'd love for her to take a day in my shoes and deal with shit like this. Silly bitch."

"Glad that you have that attitude, Your Majesty," Roberta says. "She may be a silly bitch, but she is bringing in more than her quota and I'd hate to lose her."

"Uhm," Xavi interjects and leans down. "I could give her gonorrhea if you like," she says with a small laugh.

I look up at her in amusement. "You'd do that for me?" I ask, hand on my heart.

"I would do anything for you," she murmurs. "Just think, she will go back to Earth and spread it around…" She sighs with happiness at the thought of a rampant outbreak of an STI.

I look at Roberta, who shrugs. "That is up to you," she says. "I just wanted to bring you in here to tell you that for the most part, you are doing an excellent job. Your father would be proud."

The choke that threatens to come out catches me off guard. The pang of pain over having him so close yet so far hits me hard.

I look back at Xavi. "Do it," I say. "Show this bitch reviewer just who she is messing with. Go to town. Give her crabs as well. Let her spread the joy around."

Xavi snickers and snaps her fingers. "Done," she says.

I raise an eyebrow at her efficiency.

"Her name is on the folder," she says with a laugh.

"I think I might just be falling for you," I say without even thinking about the words as I return her laugh.

She blushes. "Anything for you, Mistress," she murmurs, heating me up from the inside out.

Roberta clears her throat loudly. We both look at her, having completely forgotten she was there.

"Right," I say awkwardly, grabbing Xavi's hand.

"One more thing," Roberta says. "The lockdown…"

"Lift it," I say, feeling bright all of a sudden. "The snow has stopped. Sure, the sun is out, but it's not so unusual as to start causing chaos. I think everyone is quite aware of what will happen if they stand against me. Besides, I don't want to give Darius any more opportunity to nearly kill Aleister." It reminds me that Roberta was complicit in covering that up. I glare at her and she feels my wrath.

She looks down. "I was doing what was right for *you*. That is why I am here. You are my priority and had you seen him that way with Darius nearby, you'd have killed him. You might dislike his methods, but you need him."

"I hear you, but if anything like this happens again, it will be *your* head that I bash in with Babe. Are we clear?"

"Very," she says quietly, still not looking at me.

I grip Xavi's hand tighter and then flame out. I have nothing else to add. She gets the point.

I land outside Sid's room and knock gently. I turn to Xavi and say, "Can you give us a minute."

"Of course," she murmurs. "I'll be in my room when you want to find me."

"Downstairs!" Devlin calls to us from the top of the main staircase.

We both turn to look at him.

"Annie, we're waiting for you in the Dining Hall," he adds,

drawing his black sunglasses down to peer at me over the top of them.

"Give me a minute," I grit out and wave him and Xavi off as Sid cracks the door open.

"Annabelle."

"May I come in, please?" I ask him, not used to having such manners. I normally barge into rooms like I own them. Mostly because I *do* own them, but also because no one is really going to challenge me.

He steps back, letting me in and then closes the door quietly behind him.

"We need to talk," I say, and he nods briskly. He looks less fragile today. Stronger. More confident.

I bite my lip, hoping that this conversation will go better than yesterday's.

"I'll start," he says.

CHAPTER 24

Sid

I LOOK AT HER. My Queen. Without Leviathan in my head every second telling me that Annabelle doesn't care about me and that I'm worthless, has made me think clearly. I am out of prison. I no longer feel the burn of the fire against my skin. I'm not called upon to haunt the dreams of creatures turning them into nightmares anymore and I'm not scared to admit to the female in front of me that I love her.

I *am* still scared that she will reject me, find me hideous and not want to touch me, but I know that if I continue to push her away, I will lose her completely.

She presses those full red lips together as she waits for me to speak.

"Annabelle," I say quietly. I love her name. It is beautiful and strong just like she is.

"Sid," she says, not being able to stay silent.

It makes me smile. She is all about action. She said she was, and I know it to be true. Words don't mean as much to her as they can be lies.

That is why I'm not going to speak. I'm going to act.

In a flash of speed, I'm in front of her, taking her in my arms. I lower my mouth to hers, relieved that she tilts her head up and lets me touch my lips to hers.

"Sid," she breathes out before she wraps her arms around me and opens her mouth to delve her tongue against mine. She takes control of the kiss, as I knew she would. I want her to. I can't. It took all of my courage to initiate it. Now, I can let her do the rest.

I spent all of last night in silence, knowing that I needed to do something after our conversation yesterday. Leviathan has been true to her word and stayed away. She won't forever. She will grow bored before the three days are up and come back to torment me. I needed to work up the nerve to do this today.

And I did.

I twist my tongue around hers in a beautiful, loving kiss. I pour all of my feelings about her into this one joining of our lips. I slip my hand into her hair and moan softly. She smells like honeysuckle and tastes as sweet.

She pulls away and looks into my eyes with that slight smirk that makes hers light up. "What was that for?" she asks quietly.

"I need you to know how I feel," I whisper. "I can't say it, not yet, but I needed you to know."

"Oh, Sid," she sighs and hugs me, putting her head on my chest. "Thank you. I hate the way we left things yesterday."

"Me too. There is something I need to tell you…"

"Same," she interrupts me before I can dredge up the courage to demand that she kill Leviathan before three days are up.

"Annabelle…"

"Sid, I have something I need to tell you. I shouldn't have waited. I shouldn't have been scared about telling you. You need to hear it from me, so I need to put my selfishness aside."

She takes my face in her face, stroking my cheeks with her thumbs. She smiles at me and my heart stops.

"I love you," she whispers to me so quietly, I barely heard her. "I love you, Sid. I'm not afraid to say it to you. You bring out a part of me that needs to love. I want to protect you, keep you safe. I can't do that unless you know how much I love you. I will go to the ends of Hell and back to make sure that no one ever hurts you again. You will know that I'll protect you at all costs because I love you."

"Oh," I whimper, not daring to even take a breath. The tears well up in my eyes as she smiles at me again, that slow, sexy smile. I kiss her again. I devour her mouth with mine. I want to say the words back, but I can't speak. Not yet. She has laid her heart bare for me. *For me*. She put her own fear aside for me. The least I can do is reciprocate that trust.

"I love you, Annabelle. I trust you," I murmur to her and push her back to the bed.

She gasps as she knows what I want to do. I didn't think I would, or could so soon, if at all. I am terrified. My blood is pumping through my veins so fast, so fierce it is making me feel sick. I want her to make love to me, I want it so badly, I can taste it. I don't know how the next few minutes will go. I don't know if she will be gentle with me or throw me around the bed. I don't care. I just want her to, no, *need* her to, back up her words.

I sit on the bed and moan as she crawls into my lap, writhing against me as her tongue wraps around mine, her hands move down my body and then rip my shirt open. The buttons fly off in all directions and she pulls away from our kiss to look at me.

The hot blood in my veins goes cold.

I'm as badly scarred on my chest as I am on my face.

She lowers her mouth to the bare mutilations. I freeze. I don't push her away, I just remain trapped, motionless in time.

"Annabelle," I sob, suddenly gripping her arms and shoving her away from me. "Please, don't."

"Sid, let me love you," she croons.

I stay silent, the scream in my head demanding that I end this. I don't *want* to. I want her to keep kissing me, keep touching me. But I know that I *can't* do this. Not yet.

She pushes me back to the bed, wriggling on my lap, making my body respond to her, but my fractured mind can't deal with it. I started this, but I wasn't ready.

"I'm not ready," I say, grabbing her hands that are stroking my burn scars tenderly. "I'm sorry."

I hate myself for leading her on, making her think that I was going to share my body with her. The shame of my weakness is forever etched onto my skin. I'm not ready to let her keep seeing it, touch it, kiss it.

"Sid, I'm sorry. I'll stop," she whispers.

I can hear the disappointment in her voice.

I scrunch my eyes up wanting to tell her not to stop. I want to sink into her hot, wet haven and forget all about my pain, my darkness.

She climbs off me, her nipples so erect under her thin top, I groan with frustration at myself.

"You say that you trust me, Sid," she says, running her fingers over my twisted lips. "Trust that I will be careful with your heart and your body. I can, you know, despite what you've heard."

I look up at her in surprise. She's trying not to laugh at herself.

"I do trust you," I say, taking her hand and kissing it. "Next time, I won't stop you."

"Are you saying that it's up to me to decide when the next time is?" she asks carefully.

"I trust you," I say again. "But there are Demons in my head. She won't leave me alone."

"I will slay them for you if I can, my sweet Sid. Will you let me?"

I gulp. I need to tell her about Leviathan. Now is my chance. "She needs to be destroyed," I blurt out.

Annabelle frowns at me. "Who?"

I take in a deep breath, knowing that she will feel me say her name out loud and crush me. I have to trust Annabelle to crush her back, once and for all.

"Leviathan," I say steadily and then scream as the Demon rips through my conscious thoughts with a roar of thunder that forces me past submission and into unconsciousness.

CHAPTER 25

Annabelle

I STARE DOWN AT SID, writhing in pain on the bed, the sheer rage that builds up is making it difficult to breathe.

"You are dead, bitch," I snarl in his face, hoping she can hear me. "I'm coming for you."

Sid groans and curls up, turning his back to me. I want to stay and make sure that he is okay, but if I stay, I will only end up hurting him. Eradicating him even.

I flame out before the Shift takes me over. I land next to Leviathan's cell, my wings already unfurled and flapping wildly in my anger.

Through the red haze that is rapidly descending over my eyes, I see the orb hovering in the middle of the cell. I hold my hand out. It explodes into a million pieces, releasing the bitch.

She lands on her feet, crouched down and stands up slowly, stretching out her body luxuriously with a vicious smirk on her face as she looks at me.

"It's a start," she drawls, stalking over to the bars of the cell. "Just one more step."

"You are fucking deluded if you think you are going anywhere," I grate out.

"Release me or I will keep tormenting that pathetic creature you have grown so fond of. He is as connected to me as I am to Hell. You can't sever that. You have one choice if you want me to leave him alone."

"No, I have two choices. Your way or *my* way and you will learn pretty fucking quickly that all ways in Hell are *my* way."

"Hmm. Even if you kill me, I'll still be here. Lucifer made sure that I would never leave him."

"Too fucking bad for you then that Great-Gramps isn't here, and *I* am," I inform her before I stop fighting it and I Shift.

It starts with the back breaking, bone crunching agony before I lose every ounce of pain, every ounce of *anything*. All that is left is destruction.

My face changes shape, my jaw elongating to accommodate the goat's head of my Devil form. My tail swishes out behind me, the pointed tip razor sharp, slashing out at the bars of the cage. I grew several feet in height and bulk out until I'm twice the size of my human form. My clothes are shreds hanging off me. A quick shake discards them completely as my cloven hooves scrape on the stone floor of the prison. The only thing that remains remotely the same are my hands, except my fingers are longer with talons like knives and dripping with poison which makes the Hellfire on my fingertips flare up every now and again.

I see Leviathan's face pale as she licks her lips.

"Lucifer," she mutters and then screams as I rake my claws over the bars of her cell, and they disappear under the magick.

She stands in front of me, trembling. I don't bother

looking over my shoulder to see if she means Lucifer is behind me.

Nope. She means that *I* am Lucifer and she finally gets that. It gives me all the information I need to give to my mother. *When* I'm through with Leviathan.

As I take a step forward, I lose the shred of rational *human* thought that lingered after the Shift.

I need to annihilate; I need to make this bitch suffer before I end her reign of terror once and for all.

She shrieks in agony as I grab her by her upper arms and fling her against the dark stone wall of the prison.

The sickening crunch echoes throughout the deep cavern as her bones shatter from the force of the blow. She slides down the wall as I stamp over to her, not giving her body a second to heal before I haul her off her feet and slam her against the wall again.

"Release him," I grit out, the action of speaking in this form tearing my throat apart.

I ignore the taste of my own blood.

She laughs at me weakly, but the insult is clear. "Not a fucking chance," she rasps as my hand closes around her neck. "Kill me, but I will still be here, and I will keep him in torment for eternity. He will suffer unbelievably from my wrath…gah…"

Her words are cut short as I squeeze tightly.

"Annabelle."

I hear War's urgent voice call out to me, but I ignore it. This has nothing to do with him.

I slam Leviathan against the wall again, rattling the bones in her body. Her muffled whimper speaks to the beast in me. It riles *Her* up. *She* needs more destruction, more pain, more suffering, more torment.

"Anna!"

War's voice booms through my head, but I dismiss it.

I squeeze Leviathan's throat until I hear a crack. "RELEASE HIM!" I bellow in her face, ripping my throat apart.

"Never!" she snarls.

I throw her limp body over to the other side of the cavern, relishing every second of her hitting the wall and slumping down to the ground in a pile of blood and bones. She can't Shift. She doesn't have the strength to change her shape into that of her cat to slip out. Engulfed in flames, I appear in front of her again and drag her to her feet. I rake my talons down her face, making her scream. I draw my arm back and then ram my hand into her gut, grabbing hold of her insides and pulling them out of the cavity.

Her shrieks make me smile.

I swallow and brace myself to grate out to her, "He suffers, you suffer."

"Fuck. You," she pants.

I know that as much fun as this is for the beast, I have to end it. Sid is suffering every second I play with my prey.

That resonates in my foggy brain.

I release my hold on her and drop her guts on the floor, setting them on fire with just a thought. As she writhes around, trying to get away from the sheer torture I'm inflicting on her, I bring both of my hands up and raise her body off the floor with magick. She hangs in the air in front of me like a macabre puppet with a gaping hole in her stomach. I wave one hand over her face, burning her eyes out of the sockets as she screams.

Growing weary of the noise, I rip her tongue out of her mouth and fling it on the floor, stepping on it and crushing it underneath my hoof.

The silence is deafening. I can hear War's heavy breathing from too close to me. I need him to back off. I would hate to end him if he tries to stop me from what I'm about to do next.

"Suffer," I whisper, unable to utter a word any louder, but they both hear me, nonetheless. "Suffer for eternity."

I'm calling her bluff. Killing her will release her hold on Sid. I'm as sure of it as I can be. If I'm wrong, I will deal with it when rational thought returns. All I want right now is to damage this bitch as much as I can.

I bring my hands up and force my talons into her temples.

I barely register the keening noise that emits from her tongueless mouth.

Wiggling my fingers inside her head, I project exactly what I want to happen. She is going to die a thousand deaths, ten thousand, a hundred thousand deaths over and over again. I'm going to keep her in a loop of eternal death, killing her again and again, over and over. She will relive the moment from when I freed her from her cell to when I burn her body with the fires of Hell, scarring her body and her essence as she did to Sid. In this cycle, she will never truly die. She will never be able to haunt Hell as a specter. She will come back to life the next second after she dies, only to go through her nightmare again. There is no way she will be able to keep her hold on Sid.

I breathe out through my open mouth, fire followed by smoke curls out, a faint wisp, but it is enough to blacken her skin, melting it off her bones as her hair lights up like a Tiki-torch.

War is panting close to my ear. I can *smell* his arousal. It is emanating off him in waves of musky scent. I can feel his hot breath blowing on me.

I pull my fingers out of Leviathan's head and wiggle them, encasing her in a small fire cube where she will remain in her own horrendous nightmare forever. I throw my arm out to send the cube over to where Razor is still suffering. It hovers and grows in size and then settles.

"Anna," War rasps at me, grabbing my arm and turning me towards him.

I blink. Before me stands an enormous red horse, decked out in barding as if prepared for battle.

My gaze roams over him, climbing higher and higher as I take in the enormity of him. He stands at least twice as high as me, snorting at me and stomping his front legs.

He descends on me, pushing me back to the sacrificial altar at the end of the cavern.

I growl at him, tearing my healed throat wide open again.

I blink again and, in a flash, he is in his human form, shoving his huge hands against my chest to push me backwards.

I stumble but don't fall as he returns to his true Hell form. He doesn't have the strength to get me on my back. My wings flap wildly in irritation at his behavior, but then he nuzzles me, his horse's head going between my legs and drawing in a deep breath.

I nearly choke on the lust that drives through me. I have *never* fucked in this form. I can't. It's an impossibility as there isn't a Demon in Hell that won't be eradicated by being this close to me.

Until now.

"War," I rasp.

His intention is clear. He wants to ride my Devil as his true Hell form and I'm going to let him. There isn't a single being in creation that could stop me and even if there was... Fuck. That.

Walking backwards, I hit the altar. I hop up and lie back. I open my legs, wondering if I even *have* a pussy down there. It's never been explored.

As he flashes back to his human form, I find that I do

have a working cunt in this body. He shoves his tongue straight into it, making me buck. It becomes apparent that my Devil's cunt *hasn't* been used before to my utter shock. I'm a virgin again and the irony of it makes me snort in amusement.

My tail swipes at him, slashing his skin as it waves around in my excitement. He pays it no mind though as once again, he is towering over me in his horse form.

The rasp that tears through me echoes around the cavern. His dick has elongated into an enormous appendage that makes me shiver in anticipation.

He rears up, kicking his front legs before he mounts me.

A scream of desire tears out of my damaged throat as he flashes back to his human form. I close my eyes as he shoves his massive cock into my virgin pussy, tearing past the barrier without a bit of remorse in his driven arousal as he pounds into me.

I open my eyes again and gasp as my orgasm starts to build and I find his Hell form looking back at me.

CHAPTER 26

Devlin

I WAIT, listening to the screams and grunts. It's driving me into a state of feral destruction, but if I take a step into that cavern, I will be eradicated. It *really* grates on me that Killian gets to be in there with her. Like the big stud isn't alpha enough, now he's the only one that gets to see her true form. Her Devil form. Plus, the fact that he knows I'm standing out here with my dick in my hand makes it even more of a raw wound. Okay, so not exactly with my dick in my hand. Yet. If they keep this up, it won't be long.

I blink as Xavi swirls into view with a curious look on her face. "Where is she? I thought you two came to find her?"

"She's in there, but I wouldn't go in if I were you," I say, pointing back into the cavern. Although, if Killian can see Annabelle's Devil form, then it makes sense that Xavi can too.

"Why?" she asks with narrowed eyes and without waiting for an answer, peers around the corner.

I see her eyes go wide and she stumbles back slightly, her

hand on her stomach. "Uhm," she says and points inside. "Have you *seen* that?"

"No, sadly, I can't, love," I grit out.

She tilts her head at me and then understanding dawns. "Ooh," she murmurs. "True Devil form and all that…"

"Yeah."

"So why are you still standing here?" she asks with a smirk.

I let out a laugh. I have to admit I like this female. I don't find her attractive, not in the sex sense. She's got a face you can look at, which is saying a lot down here. But her feisty attitude, the fact that she is smitten with Annie and her sass is a good package for our Queen. I can see why she swung the other way on this one.

"What can I say?" I chuckle. "I'm a sucker for punishment."

She laughs back. "You don't say. You're staying?"

"Yeah. I have a feeling that the crash will be pretty steep after this high," I say, the worry of that making my face go dark.

"Hmm," she murmurs. "I will stay too."

"Actually, would you go and tell the others that the meeting is fucked. We'll have to catch up later."

She hesitates, her lips pressed together, but then says, "Sure." She swirls back out.

I don't feel bad for making her go. I'm here. I've been here since Annie started her revenge on Leviathan. I want to be here for her when she burns out. By the sounds of it, it will be quite soon.

Her voice has changed. She is back in her human form and Killian is murmuring to her. I take that as my cue to duck into the cavern.

I walk steadily past the two huge firecubes and swallow as my mouth has gone dry. Sid said something about these being used as her ninth circle. Hearing what she did to Leviathan, I have to wonder who the fuck is in the other one and what they did to the Demon Queen to deserve it.

"Is she okay?" I croak out. The air in here is full of ash and brimstone. I can *see* it.

"No," Killian says, sweeping her up into his arms to cradle her gently. "She is worn out."

"Crashed, I get it."

"Something like that," he mutters, giving me a scrutinizing glare. "You stayed?"

"I did," I say, glaring back at him.

"You heard?"

"Oh, yeah," I inform him.

He doesn't seem overly concerned about that, so I don't say any more. I really wish I'd seen what Xavi had. Perhaps she will have to explain it to me in graphic detail. I doubt very much that I'll get anything out of Killian.

My eyes drop to Annie, limp in Killian's arms. "Has she passed out?" I ask, going to her and stroking her hair.

"Yes," Killian says. "Don't get any ideas."

My eyes flick back up to his. "What are you talking about?"

He sneers at me. "I know about the darkness inside you, Necro. Don't think for a second that you will get your hands on her in this state."

I balk at him, insulted. "Fuck you, arsehole," I snarl at him. "What the fuck do you think I am?"

"I know that you wanted her held down while you fucked her. I also know that she enjoyed it and has probably asked you to take it to the next level, however that may work. Something to do with her powerless body, maybe?"

I growl at him. How the fuck does he know that? Annie whispered that to *me*. The other men didn't hear it. I know they didn't. They would've had something to say, no doubt.

159

"You have no idea what you're talking about," I say stiffly. It's not up to me to tell him what Annie said to me in a private moment. If she wants him to know, she can tell him herself. Something tells me though, she doesn't or she would have.

His sneer deepens, curling his lip up at me. "Like I said, I know about the darkness in you," he says and then with a bolt of lightning, he vanishes with Annie.

I grimace and follow them, knowing he'll have taken her to her bedroom.

I'm right.

He is tucking her up in bed when I get there.

He ignores me for a minute, but then he stalks over to me and grabs my arm. He hauls me out of the bedroom and drags me down the hallway to mine.

I can't stop him. I'm about a foot shorter than him for a start and nowhere near his level of power.

He kicks the door open and shoves me inside. "I told you, you aren't going anywhere near her."

"I don't fuck unconscious bodies," I snarl at him, thoroughly affronted by his insinuation.

"No?" he asks. "You want them awake but completely still? Or is it the dead you prefer to stick your dick into?"

My hands clench into two fists that are aching to beat the shit out of him. Sadly, I would lose that fight. But it doesn't fucking stop me from launching myself at him.

"You arsehole!" I roar.

He catches my flying fist in his hand and shoves me backwards. Luckily for my pretty face, he doesn't retaliate.

"That's a fucking insulting thing to assume, dickhead," I say stiffly.

"I have known more Necros than you can count, little shit. It's not a wrong assumption to make," he states, folding his arms across his chest.

"Maybe, but have a higher opinion of me. I wouldn't come to Annie and fuck her after I'd fucked a dead person. That's pretty sick, even for me." I can't help the indignation.

"Humph," he mutters.

We glare at each other for a few seconds, neither of us moving a muscle.

"Tell me something, what did you mean when you said that it didn't surprise you in the least?" he asks, switching subjects.

I regard him closely. I know what he means, but I play it coy anyway, seeing as he *really* wants to know something from me. "What do you mean?"

His eyes narrow and he takes a step forward. "Six hundred and sixty-six strokes. What do you know?"

I remain silent, just to piss him off further. What can I say, I'm a fucking Anarchist.

When his next step forward, which brings him into my personal space, is way more menacing than his last, I lick my lips. His eyes drop momentarily to my mouth, catching me by surprise.

"I don't know much," I huff, "But you might want to sit down before I start."

CHAPTER 27

Annabelle

I GROAN, putting my hand to my forehead, I risk cracking an eye open.

It's light out, sunny and cheerful. I want it to fuck off.

"Annabelle," Gregory's voice registers in my foggy brain. "How're you feeling?"

"Like shit on a stick," I growl softly. "What happened?"

"Killian told us that you exacted revenge on Leviathan in your true Devil form. It wiped you out," he says.

I shut my eyes again with a low moan. Is that what he said? Clearly, he forgot to add the depraved mating we engaged in afterwards. My eyes fly open. "How's Sid?" I ask, sitting up and ignoring the protesting thump in my head.

"He is resting," he says carefully.

"What does that mean?" I bark at him.

"He isn't in any pain that we can see. We aren't really sure what happened, only that Leviathan had something to do with it. So, it's hard to tell what's going on with him."

I flop back to the bed. He was in torment when I left.

They would've been able to see if he was still in that state. I smile, remembering what I did to that bitch. I will find it difficult not to pull her out of the loop in a few month's time to see how she is getting on.

"Help me up," I order Gregory. "I need to shower and go see him."

"Do you feel up to it?" he ventures.

I sit up again. "I'm the Demon Queen," I say haughtily. "One Shift isn't going to put me down for long." To prove it, I clamber off the bed, naked and sore. I smile secretly. Killian was magnificent. It was an experience that I won't forget in a hurry. We will need to repeat it very soon, with Elijah in his Hellhound form, for good measure. Of course, I won't be able to Shift if Elijah is there, but I'm pretty sure this body can handle it. I stagger into the bathroom, leaving Gregory sitting on my bed, watching me.

I still can't believe that my Devil form was a virgin. I mean, come the fuck on. That is just a fucking joke waiting to happen. I giggle to myself and step into the shower, turning it on.

My mood soon turns sour as I remember the damned box. Somehow, I'm going to have to convince my mother that she needs to give it to me. Everyone seems to have forgotten that opening it doesn't release Lucifer. He is *still* in the depiction. He has to be released from that before he is out and about, and there isn't a single creature here that will oblige him.

So, fuck him, basically.

I stick my head under the torrent of water and close my eyes.

I turn my head as I hear the bathroom door open and then the shower door slides to the side.

"Gregory," I say, giving him a raised eyebrow and a lusty look.

He is completely naked.

"We got cut short the other day," he says.

"We did," I agree, turning to face him full on.

His eyes drop to my cunt and then up to linger on my tits. The heat in his eyes makes me damp.

I move over to make room for him, and he steps inside, quietly sliding the door closed.

I look up at him and notice that he is a bit taller than I thought. I'm used to being in six-inch heels around him, not my bare feet.

We don't say a word as his hands go into my hair and he pulls me closer to him, kissing me deeply and slowly.

I shiver under his gentle touch. I've always known that I wouldn't get rough and ready with him. He is human and fairly innocent. I knew that he would always take the soft approach.

What surprises me, is that I let him.

I have absolutely no need to slam him through the shower door and onto the bathroom floor to mount him and ride him like a cowgirl. Whatever he has planned for me, I want it and I'm willing to wait for it.

I kiss him back just as slowly, enjoying the simple act for itself. I couldn't care less if we fucked now or not. Although, judging by his raging hard-on, it would have to take Hell falling down around our ears for him to stop now. It has probably taken a lot of courage for him to come to me like this, and I want to enjoy him completely.

He pushes me up against the black tiles, stepping under the torrent now and getting drenched as our lips remain locked together in a heated exchange. Our tongues are perfectly in sync, twirling around each other. I grip his forearms, trying not to crush him in the process.

"Gregory," I breathe as he moves his mouth away from mine to trail down my jaw and neck.

He responds by bringing his hands to my tits and tweaking my nipples. There isn't anything salacious in it at all. It is sensual as fuck and my body reacts to his touch in a way that I have never experienced before.

He bends down to suck one of my nipples into his mouth. I run my hands into his hair and let my head fall back against the tiles as I arch my back.

When his hand snakes down my stomach and in between my legs, I gasp. He rubs my clit once before plunging his finger into me and then back out again to tease me.

"Fuck," I murmur. "Fuck, yes."

It is slow, sexy and the fact that we are standing in the shower doing it adds a whole new level of eroticism to the moment. I don't want it to end.

I blink as that thought crashes into my head, dousing my arousal in a big way. He is being this way because he is *human.* If I turn him into a Necro, he will lose his humanity and pull the darkness over him. He won't be able to help it. It will be natural for him. It makes me seriously reconsider my plan. Only, that doesn't leave me many options.

I cry out as his attention to my pussy gets the better of me, scattering my thoughts. He drops to his knees and delves his tongue down my slit, flicking over my still throbbing clit in deliciously slow movements.

I shove my hands into his hair, resisting the urge to steer him where I want him to go, which is a tiny bit lower so he can give me a tongue-fucking that I'll remember for a really long time. As if he can read my thoughts, he does precisely that in the next second, pulling my leg over his shoulder.

"Unholy fuck," I pant as he thrusts his tongue up my cunt, that he now has unfettered access to. He is lapping up my juices as if it's the best thing he has ever tasted.

"Annabelle," he murmurs. "You taste so sweet."

"Let me suck you off," I mutter.

He shakes his head. "No, if I come too soon, that will be it for a while," he says with a small laugh. "Let me make love to you this time."

Make love.

The words reverberate around my head. I don't think I have *ever* made love before. I fuck. I have sex, even mating now, but not even Drescal and I engage in *making love*. It is a whole new concept and I like it.

A lot.

Gregory gently lowers my leg as he stands up again and wraps his arms around me. I jump up and he braces me against the wall. I wrap my legs around him tightly, clinging to him as we kiss again. I can taste my cum on his lips.

I wiggle, taking his cock in my hand, enjoying the size and weight of it against my palm. "Oh, yes," I whisper and guide it into me.

He takes over, forcefully thrusting into me until he is balls deep but then he pauses. He withdraws enough to keep just his tip inside and then he slides all the way back in slow as fuck.

"Uhn!" I moan as he continues to torture me with this move. Where did he learn this stuff? He said he'd fucked only two women in his life. One of them must've shown this tactic to bring a female to the edge of an explosion and teeter on the brink of it. My pussy is throbbing, but I haven't come yet. It's there, at my fingertips, but it's being an evasive fucker.

As he starts to speed up, burying his dick deeper into me, it hits me like Babe against a Demon's soft head.

Every nerve-ending pings as my climax zaps through me like lightning.

"Oh, fuck, yes! Yes!" I scream as my pussy clutches wildly at his dick. I dig my sharp nails into his back, making him grunt. "Again!" I pant. "Please!"

To my utmost disappointment, he pulls all the way out

and takes my hand. He opens the shower door and steps out, bringing me with him. His cock is bouncing in front of him covered in my cum as he leads me back into the bedroom. He crawls onto the bed, drawing me close to him and turning me to face away from him. Thinking we are about to get it on Hellhound-style, I shiver, but instead he lays me down and curls up around me. He lifts my leg to place over his and then he guides his dick inside me again. His fingers start to play with my clit. Circling, flicking, swirling, pinching, rubbing, twisting as he pounds into me.

"Shit, shit," he pants, and I know he is close.

I push my backside closer to him, wanting to feel him pour his load into me, when the door opens and Devlin walks in, saying, "Annie, we need to talk."

"Dev!" I cry out, for once not wanting anyone else to get involved. This is way too perfect, just the two of us.

Gregory groans and if it's possible, I feel him get even harder inside me as he glances at Devlin.

Oh?

I look over my shoulder at him, but he is focused solely on his task now to make us both burst into flames of desire.

"Err," Devlin mutters, but doesn't go anywhere. In fact, he closes the door and sits in the armchair in the corner of the room.

He pulls his dick out as Gregory slams into me, pulling on my hips as he keeps up his clit-teasing until I clench so hard around him, he grunts in surprise which turns to delight as he feels my cum soaking his dick thoroughly.

He glances at Devlin as he pumps and pounds, his breathing getting even heavier as he watches the Necromancer jerk himself off while he watches us making love.

Devlin stands and moves closer, holding one hand up as the other is wrapped around his dick, tugging fiercely. "Not touching, just wanna...uhh..." He spurts his load on my tits groaning deeply. Gregory draws in a sharp breath and then with one last thrust, his cock detonates inside me, releasing a stream of cum that mixes with mine and slides back out onto the black satin sheets.

"Jesus, fuck," he pants.

Devlin snorts with humor as I turn to give him an incredulous look.

"Sorry," Gregory pants with a laugh, "Sorry, but Christ on a bike, Annabelle. That was incredible."

"Oh, you don't need to convince me," I murmur, once again feeling that I will lose this part of him when I turn him into a creature of Hell.

I don't want that.

It makes this situation a whole Hell of a lot more complicated than it should have been.

He withdraws from me and flops back to the bed, still rasping.

I exchange a look with Devlin and somehow, he seems to get what I'm thinking as his mouth goes up at one side and he shrugs. He stashes his cock back in his pants and regards us as he sits on the bed.

"That was fucking hot," he remarks.

"We made love," I tell him, trying the words out loud.

His baby blues focus on mine intently. "I can see that," he says.

I rip my gaze away from his and turn to Gregory.

He is asleep.

I smile and stroke his cheek with the back of my hand.

I look back at Devlin as I climb off the bed. "What am I going to do with him?" I ask, not really expecting an answer.

Which, as it turns out, is a good thing because there is a knock at the door and my mother walks in without waiting for a reply, carrying the box.

She purses her lips at me and rolls her eyes skyward. "Get

dressed, baby girl. You have bigger things to concentrate on right now."

"On it," I say with a smirk, snapping my fingers to clothe myself. I flick the covers over Gregory but wave my hand over him at the same time, sending him back to his room where he can sleep off his fuck-hangover in peace.

CHAPTER 28

Shax

I STARE at Pandora's Box, hovering in the corner of Belle's room. I absently stroke Mouse's right head while Belle strokes her left. She called me in here a while ago and we've been standing here since.

"So, how come Mom gave it back to you?" I ask after a long, very meaningful pause.

Belle sighs. "Apparently, War is a bit of a chatty fucker. The whole of Hell knows what I did to Leviathan, including Mom. The details were quite precise and therefore she now feels that I'm capable of defending not only myself, but you, the unborn baby and her from Lucifer, should he pop out of that box when you open it. *Not* that I think he will. He is in the depiction. I can't see any version of events where he managed to get out of it while being locked up. I don't touch it when I pull my dad's painting out of there, then all good. We will lock it back up and you destroy it. Is that all, or do you want me to go on?"

"Nope, got it," I say, and we go back to staring at the box. "So, we doing this now?"

"Yep."

I nod and pull the regular dagger out of the back of my pants. Since I've come back here, I haven't felt the need to cut myself. The battle of dark and light in me has finally been won. I belong here and I'm fine with that.

I take a deep breath and with a quick glance at Belle, who is holding her hands out ready to either fight or grab Luc's painting, I slash my palm and drop it on the lock.

With bated breath, we wait, but absolutely fuck all happens. Much like when Belle tried to open it with the key.

"Well, that's anticlimactic – again," she says, pursing her lips. "Oh, wait!" She holds out her palm and the key to the box appears. "Here, smear some blood on this," she adds and grabs my hand to roughly swipe the key over it.

"Uhm," I say indignantly as she inserts the key into the lock.

"Dammit," she mutters. "Are you sure Vazna said it was your blood?"

"Yep."

"Fuck!" She kicks the box, but it doesn't move.

Her aggression sets off Musmortus. She starts to growl and snap her jaws. I pull my hand out of her line of sight in case she decides to chomp it off in her agitation.

"What about if I add *my* blood," Belle murmurs. "Give me the dagger."

I hand it to her wordlessly.

She slashes her palm and adds her blood to mine on the key and tries again.

"Oh, for the love of everything unholy," she snarls. "This is getting ridiculous. It *has* to be something to do with your blood *and* the key, or why would Dad go to all the trouble of hiding it with Elijah?"

"Elijah's blood?" I mutter. Belle's eyes land on me with interest. "Maybe."

"I'll go and find him," she says decisively.

I nod and let her go, wandering back to my own room. I'm suddenly feeling a little anxious about this. It is proving to be difficult to open this fucking thing. Maybe, it's because I can't. Maybe I can only destroy it.

I bite my lip and drop to my knees. I peer under the bed and draw out the box that's underneath it, picking it up and putting it on the bed. I smirk as it wasn't pushed back as far as it should've been. That means that Belle peeked. It's nothing she hasn't seen before, but I'm guessing she never expected to see them under my bed. I rummage through the box of strap-ons and butt plugs, until I find the plain glass vial filled with purple crystals. I clutch it, tapping the small cork stopper with my thumb.

I shove the vial in the pocket of my jeans, and I'm about to replace the box when there is a tap on the door I didn't close, totally forgetting that the residence is now swarming with Belle's males.

"You wanted to see me?" Elijah asks, leaning in the doorway.

I frown at him. Damn Belle. Why didn't she just tell him what we want from him?

As I scowl at him, his eyes drop to the box and linger far longer than I'd have expected. I resist the urge to hastily remove it, thus casting more suspicion onto this situation. So, I like to be fucked in the ass. So, what? Sure, I haven't quite worked up the courage to try it with a male, but getting the more depraved female Demons to strap on a dildo and ass fuck me on occasion works for me.

Elijah's eyes flick to mine as I glare defiantly at him. He licks his lips, clearly having pieced together why I have these. I feel a slight flush heat up my cheeks even though he doesn't say anything, he just clears his throat and says gruffly, "Something about my blood…"

"Uh-huh," I grunt. "Belle wants to mix ours to try and open the box."

"I see," he murmurs. "Anything for our Queen. Which brings me to another issue, while I'm here. We should clear the air."

"What air?" I ask confused.

"We left things awkwardly when you took the key from me," he points out with a tut.

"Oh, that." I brush it off with a wave of my hand. "Nothing to clear up."

He nods slowly. "So, my blood?"

"I'll meet you in Belle's room. I just have something to do first." I can hear an incessant tapping on the glass of my window behind the drawn black curtains.

"Sure," he says and disappears.

I turn quickly to the window and yank the curtains open. Shadow is there in her Griffin form, rapping her beak on the glass as she flaps her wings wildly.

I quickly open the window and she Shifts in mid-air before she leaps onto the windowsill. "Come in," I say with a smile.

"Hey," she says, tilting her mouth up for me to kiss.

I enjoy her lips on mine for a moment. The panic I'd felt when Belle told me she'd died when Vazna banished her was something that I hope I will never feel again. It hadn't taken me long to find her, and with the lockdown lifted, she is free to roam now.

"Uhm, we need to talk," she says, looking down at the box on my bed. Shadow doesn't know about my anal activities. I have never asked her to wear a strap on and I never will. I don't want that from her.

"It's…" I start, taking the box and dropping it on the floor to kick under the bed.

She shakes her head, holding her hand up. "Shax. Bannister has finally chosen his mate," she blurts out. "It's me."

I feel the ice in my veins at her words. The Head Griffin has chosen her to be his mate.

"Tell him no," I say stiffly. "Tell him you are with me."

"He doesn't know about my human side," she stammers. "I can't tell him no. It's not how it works."

"Then I shall change the way it works," I spit out, unreasonably angry with her for not trying harder to get out of this.

"Shax," she says desperately. "You can't…"

"Can't I? My sister is Queen. She can do whatever the fuck she wants, and she wants me to be happy. Unless this is something that you…want?" I swallow loudly as she doesn't answer me. Her yellow eyes go wider as she fails to say anything.

"I see," I say quietly.

"No," she says, shaking her head. "It's not that…"

"Forget it. Go and be his mate. I have shit to do right now. I don't have time for you and your drama."

I know I'm being harsh on her, but I can't help it. I'm hurt. After everything we went through, I thought she'd finally come around.

"Shax, please," she calls out as I leave the room, pulling the vial out of my pocket as I go. The crystallized Bacchus Demon blood is a strong drug that will dull the pain of this. I wanted it at first to ease my anxiety over the box. But now, now I need it to forget.

I push open the door to Belle's room to find it empty. I cross over to the box and glare at it, popping a few crystals into my mouth.

I sit down on the floor and wait for oblivion, along with Belle and Elijah, wherever the fuck they are.

CHAPTER 29

Drescal

I PICK at the food on the platter in front of me. Needing a bit of headspace, I escaped into the Dining Hall a few moments ago. I'm not used to living with so many creatures. It's going to take a bit of getting used to.

"Oh. I'll come back."

I look up at Gregory's voice. He walked into the Dining Hall and stopped dead, giving me a wary look. I don't blame him. I was an ass to use my magick on him. I'd apologized to him briefly when we spoke with Devlin about his options, but he is still clearly cautious.

"No, sit, please," I say, kicking out the chair to my left.

The scrape of the heavy wood on the stone floor echoes through the room.

"Okay," he says and moves forward, sinking into the chair when he reaches it.

As soon as he sits down, a big silver platter appears in front of him with a domed lid over the top.

I'm curious to see what he ordered from the kitchen. I

ordered a bunch of stuff I can pick at because I don't really need to eat, I just wanted something to do.

I try not to gape at the massive sandwiches piled up. There is also a side salad, chips and chocolate cake.

"Hungry," he says and dives in, picking up a sandwich and taking a big bite.

"Must be nice," I say wistfully.

He looks at me, chewing thoughtfully. "You don't get hungry?"

I shake my head. "I don't enjoy food either. I always wondered what it would be like to eat all that…" I gesture at his platter, "and taste it, savor it, you know."

He nods slowly. "It's not the same, but I had this really shitty cold once, I couldn't taste a thing."

I snort in amusement as he caught me off guard with his humor. "No, not exactly the same," I agree.

We fall into a comfortable silence as he eats.

He polishes off his first sandwich and looks at me again. "Want to talk about it?" he asks.

"What makes you think I have something to talk about?" I reply.

"It's my job," he retorts. "Here if you need to," he adds and picks up his second sandwich.

I hesitate. I *could* do with someone to talk to. I remember that Killian went to him to ask him about how to handle Anna once before. Maybe this could throw up something that will, if not help me, make me feel less like the weight of the world is on my shoulders.

"It's complicated," I start.

He shrugs. "When is it not?"

I nod. That's probably true.

"Just so we are clear, this stays between us, yeah?"

"Of course," he says.

"Also, this isn't me *complaining*," I point out, stabbing my finger on the table so he gets that I'm being serious about that part.

"I get it," he says lightly.

I sigh and sit back.

He goes back to eating and it helps that he doesn't focus on me. I'm more inclined to blurt it out if he is looking at his sandwich.

"I've been an Incubus for nine hundred years," I start.

He nods, but doesn't say anything.

"I was *made* this way. Came through with my Reaper, recycled and here I am."

He nods again.

"I loved being what I was. I was the *best* at it. I loved my life on Earth. I hated being recalled, hated what I was missing out on. But then I saw Anna from across the room, wrapped around Devlin and I wanted her. *Really* wanted her. I didn't just want to fuck her. I didn't want her to be another conquest, just another female in the hundreds of thousands that I've fucked…"

Gregory chokes slightly on that and I smile. I can't help but wonder how many females are on *his* list. I wonder if Annabelle is one of them yet.

"I got to know her while I was here. She was fierce and full of fire. She had absolutely no inhibitions, she was up for anything. She fulfilled me on a level that I didn't even know existed. Yet, I had to leave her, fuck Earth's females, damn them to Hell, come back and see her, spend time with her, fall more in love with her, and then leave her again. It was a vicious cycle that tore me up. I knew that as soon as I was out of her sphere, she forgot me, took other lovers and didn't give me a second thought."

Gregory is chewing slowly now as he watches me spill my secrets.

"I was so much of a sap around her, her father even

noticed. We were friends, Luc and me. *Are* friends," I amend. "He knew me well and he could see how much I loved Anna. When he confronted me, I expected him to tear me a new one. I seriously thought the end of my days had arrived. But he wasn't mad," I say with a small laugh. "Well, not any more mad than a father of a daughter can be, I suppose. He told me he knew what it was like to be in love with someone like me, and he told me that there wasn't even the tiniest shred of hope that Anna would accept what I did, just as he didn't accept Axelle being a Seductress anymore. He told me about their relationship, how he knew that accepting her other men went a long way to keep her urges in check. But he also said that it wouldn't work the other way around. Annabelle wouldn't be one of several women that I kept around and apart from that fact, he *would not let her be*." I snort as those words were said forcefully and with Luc's hand wrapped around my throat. "I asked him to help me, to tear the Incubus out of me and let me be with her."

I stop speaking now as I have Gregory's full attention. He has abandoned his sandwich and is staring intently at me.

"And did he?" he asks after an exceptionally long pause. "You'll forgive me if I can't tell."

"No, he didn't. He said he couldn't," I say with a sigh. "He said removing the Incubus from me would just plain old remove *me* from existing. I've never felt so…" I punch my gut to make my point.

"Yeah, I get that feeling," Gregory murmurs.

I nod and take a breath. "He did, however, have a solution. One that I took without even a second thought. I knew he was right about Anna. I knew that I had to quit what I was if I had any chance of her agreeing to be with me."

"What did he suggest?" Gregory prompts me, so engrossed in my story, it makes me smile.

"He said I would have to remain an Incubus but that he could redirect my focus."

"How?" Gregory asks.

"The 'how' isn't important. I won't go into details, but it wasn't the most pleasant experience. Anyway, he redirected my focus onto Anna. I think he was partly punishing me for screwing his daughter, maybe, I dunno. Maybe he was trying to genuinely help me. He *did* help me. Like I said, I'm not complaining. I owe him everything because I can give Anna what she needs. I can give her my absolute fidelity when it comes to other females."

"I'm not sure I understand," he says with a frown.

I sigh again. "Luc made me focus only on Anna, with her blood. She is the only female that this Incubus can be with."

"Oh!" Gregory exclaims. "Really? You don't desire to be with other women anymore?"

"Nope," I say and sit back.

"Interesting," he mutters. "But how do *you* feel about that?"

"Well, that's the burning question, Doc. I feel great about it. It got me what I want. Annabelle. She is the only thing that matters, and therein lies the root of my frustration. She is the *only* thing that matters. If I'm not fucking her it eats at me. It claws at me. I need it. I need *her*. All of the time. Sharing her in the way that we are, not getting her undivided attention, rubs salt on it. I'm *not* complaining," I reiterate. "But that's the way it is."

I feel a bit lighter now that this secret is out. Not that he can help me but just having talked about it eases the burden.

"Does she know?" he asks.

"No and she won't," I say menacingly. "This is *my* issue to deal with. I won't put worry on her because of something that *I* did."

"I understand that," he says. "But you require her one-on-

one, an all-out seduction that will appease your hunger for her."

"You get it," I breathe out.

"I do, more than you know," he says carefully. "Plan something for later. Just the two of you. Arrange a romantic dinner, flirt with her, seduce her. She will appreciate the effort and it will excite her to go on a date."

"You seem to know her well considering you have been here so little time," I point out.

"I do know her," he says and goes back to the sandwich.

"Thanks," I murmur. "You've helped me."

"Happy to help," he says and then drops his sandwich as a screech of epic proportions reverberates throughout the residence. We share a panicked look, and grabbing his arm, I transport us to the source of the scream.

CHAPTER 30

Annabelle

"Shax!" I shriek at him, covering my eyes. Oh, my eyes! I don't think that I can go on with them still in my head. "What the fuck are you doing, you little shit!"

He grunts as I back out of my bedroom, stepping on Elijah's toes as I go.

"I'm going to have to burn my sheets!" I scream, slamming the door and shutting the image of my twin fucking his Griffin-in-human-form pet on my bed. "Asshole!" I shout and kick the door for good measure.

"What's going on?" Drescal asks as he turns up with Gregory, which I find curious.

I shudder. "I just...I can't..."

Elijah explains it for me. "Shax and his friend are fucking on Annabelle's bed."

I moan as my ears burn.

"Sorry!" Shax says, yanking the door open.

Thankfully, he is fully clothed. She isn't though, I note as I shove him roughly out of my way.

"We were making up…"

"Don't want to know. Don't ever use my room again for your sexcapades. It's gross!"

"I know, I'm sorry," he says again. "It was sudden and…" He runs his hand through his hair, giving Shadow a lingering look. "…complicated," he finishes up.

"Well, take your complications elsewhere. I want Elijah to try and open this box," I huff.

Shax nods and takes Shadow by the arm, leading her back to his bedroom. "Stay here. Please, don't go until we can talk more," he says.

She nods and he closes the door.

When he comes back into my room, I can see that his eyes are slightly wild, and he looks agitated, but I don't have time to worry about him.

"Box," I point to it as he falters slightly.

"Oh, yeah," he says and shakes his head as if to clear it.

Drescal and Gregory inch closer, as Killian arrives with Aleister close behind him and then Xavi. Last to arrive is Devlin and then we are all assembled except for Sid. I was with him a moment ago, making sure he was doing okay. He was still asleep, but appeared to be at peace as Gregory said earlier. When all of this is over, I'm going to spend some real time with him.

My room is now really crowded and all I can focus on is the rumpled bed, so I clear my throat and say, "Let's take this to the sin bin." I don't wait for an answer as I grab the box from where it is floating in the corner and flame out downstairs, leaving everyone to follow. I hope that someone remembers to bring Gregory.

Drescal does. He is standing quite close to my human, whether to protect him from the box or another reason, I'm glad that he is making friends here with my males.

I let go of the box next to the 'fucking rack', as I've come to think of it. It will always hold fond memories of Killian accepting that we needed to be together after he got me good on it.

"So, let's try this again and we don't give up until it's done. Got it?" I snarl at everyone.

They all nod back.

"Oh, and one more thing," I say, holding up my hand. "If you see my wings pop out...run!" I give them a bright smile and get a few snickers in return.

"Yes, Ma'am," Devlin says.

"Okay. Shax. You bleed on the key and then Elijah, you too."

I can see the puzzled looks, but I don't stop to explain. I pull the key out of my back pocket and hold it out to Shax.

To our surprise, it zips out of my hand, heading straight towards Elijah, smacking him in the forehead before it hovers in front of his face

"Ow, you bitch," he snarls at me. "You could've given me some warning."

I hold my hands up. "Wasn't me, asshole," I remark. "It went to you on its own. You *are* connected to this damn thing. I think you need to be the one to turn the key."

Suddenly, it makes perfect sense. That's why he had it in the first damn place.

He grunts an apology at me – I think – and grabs the hovering key.

Shax slashes his palm again and bleeds over the held-out piece of iron.

"Put it in the lock and turn it, but don't flip the lid," I say to him. "I'll do the honors."

"Not a problem," he mutters and inserts the key into the lock.

There is a soft sizzle and a stream of smoke filters up into the air. I hold my breath as Elijah slowly turns it to the right.

The silence is deafening.

We hear a soft *click*.

"Step back," I murmur to him.

He backs away, gripping Shax by the arm to force him to move back with him.

I step forward, my hands outstretched.

I jump a fucking mile when Gregory sneezes.

"Sorry," he whispers when I give him a death stare.

Grimly, I turn back to the box.

I carefully place my hands on the lid and lift it gingerly until it is all the way open.

I gasp as I see the portrait of my Dad propped up in front of another one and next to a small black, wrought iron box.

I swallow. I have to be super cautious now. I cannot touch the other painting.

I reach out with my index finger pointed.

"Wait," Killian says, stepping up next to me. "Let me."

"No," I say forcefully. "You said you would defer to me unless we are fucking. Is your dick in my pussy now, War? This is *my* responsibility. All I need from *you* is to protect everyone else if all Hell breaks loose in a moment. Can you do that, War? Can you defer and let me do this?"

He nods briefly and steps back. "Yes, my Queen," he mutters.

I turn back to the box and stick my finger on the frame of my father's portrait. I push it forward and draw my hand back quickly. It thunks against the front of the box making everyone, including me, jump nervously.

"Wow, that is fuck ugly," I state, looking at the ancient depiction of Lucifer. "Sorry, Great-Gramps. Not today," I add, and yank my dad's portrait out of the box quickly and slam the lid closed.

"Shax! Burn it! Now!" I shout at him as a whirlwind whips up out of nowhere, causing everyone except me to scatter to the four corners of the large room. The painting explodes just as I see a flash of lightning through the glass ceiling of the sin bin, followed by a clap of thunder. I look up to see the sky has gone dark with rain clouds and it starts to lash down, bouncing off the glass noisily.

I look back in front of me and my father appears, his face as thunderous as the sky up above.

"Annabelle Pandora!" he bellows, making me gulp on automatic reflex. "You are in for a world of trouble, young lady!"

Through the noise of the rain outside and the whirling wind inside, the snort of amusement coming from Killian echoes through the sin bin. I ignore my father's scolding and fling myself at him, shouting, "Daddy! You're home!"

CHAPTER 31

Annabelle

MY DAD SQUEEZES me tightly but then he plants me back on my feet with an expression that makes me wither.

Not the best look for me with my circle surrounding me.

Luckily, he includes Shax in on his fury. "You should have destroyed the box!" he roars. "Why did you open it?"

"To release you! Obviously!" I roar back, pissed off that he is so eager to die. It hurts.

"Dammit, Belle," he says, calming down slightly and putting his fist to his mouth. "That isn't going to work," he adds, indicating the burning box. "It was an either-or deal."

"What do you mean?" Shax asks.

"I put it in the letter," Dad snaps. "Your blood will either open the box or destroy it. You *must* destroy it." He pauses. "I wish I'd never told you the first part."

"I didn't read that as either-or,' Shax snaps back.

My father turns to face the box full on. "We cannot destroy it now that it has been opened."

"Not a problem," I state coldly. "I have a back-up plan, a nice little firecube where it can live for eternity."

Dad sighs. "If only it was that simple. You are the Anti-Christ, Annabelle. You are what he has strived for. Your power, your *essence*, being so close to him now… I fear…"

He looks at the box as it starts to spin around and around like it's possessed.

I snort at my less than amusing thought, earning myself a filthy look from Dad.

"Why didn't you say all of this in the letter?" Shax asks, raising his voice over the growing storm.

I feel the first drops of rain fall on my head as it arrives indoors, and I look up. The cloistered feeling that suddenly descends on the room makes it difficult to breathe and a wet heat makes me start to sweat.

Fanning myself, as this is most unusual inside the residence, where the scorched heat from outdoors remains there. I see my long red hair frizz up into a disgusting mess.

"Ugh!" I complain, grabbing a fistful and glaring at it.

"Are you saying that he is about to come out of the box?" Killian asks loudly, stepping closer to me and pointing at it.

"Yes," Dad says through gritted teeth, ignoring Shax's question. "Stay behind me," he orders me, giving me a shove backwards with his arm outstretched.

"Erm," I interject, stepping around his arm as I glare up at him. "*I* am the Devil now, thank you very much. I will deal with this."

"Get back," he hisses at me.

Killian's hand snakes out and grabs mine, pulling me back as the box shatters in an explosion of fireworks that burn my eyes.

"Get Gregory out of here!" I shriek as this is happening now and I need him safe. I don't stop to see if someone removed him, I'm just going to assume that they did.

The heat ripples out from where the box exploded. Xavi steps up next to me, flanking me as is Killian.

It kinda pisses me off.

It's sweet, don't get me wrong, but I can kick both of their asses along with Lucifer's *and* my dad's if I have to. Oh, and also my loser grandfather's. I think that's him in the tiny black box. Well, *was*. I'm pretty sure it will have been destroyed now.

I take a step forward when the surge of searing heat blows my hair back and dries it instantly, even though the rain is still pouring out of the roof.

It *really* fucks me off when Killian and Xavi move forward with me.

"Back off," I snarl and then everything goes quiet.

The rain stops, although the thunder clouds remain hovering high above us. The heat sizzles out and then he is there.

I take an inadvertent step back.

I'd expected a massive beast, livid and foaming at the mouth.

Instead, we all eyeball a man with my twin's father's Angelic face.

A *naked* man, that is.

"Uhm," I stammer, trying to look anywhere but down. He looks exactly like my stepfather. I just...can't!

Speaking of my stepfather, he swoops into the room, his wings flapping wildly as he lands, with my mother and Evan a second behind and appearing next to Dad.

Dad's eyebrows skyrocket at her pregnant appearance, but it doesn't stop him from taking her hand tightly and kissing it before he turns back to Great-Gramps. I can see everyone is coiled as tight as a cobra ready to strike.

"Well," Lucifer says, brushing his light blonde hair out of his forest green eyes. He steps forward and fortunately, clothes himself with a shimmer of power, choosing to dress exactly like my dad in a black shirt and black jeans. I figure it's because when he died, clothing was a HellBear-skin smock, so he went with what he saw.

No one breathes a word as Lucifer takes another step forward. "Some of you I know," he says icily, his gaze landing on Killian and Xavi. "Most of you are new," he adds, casting his gaze over the assembled crowd. I can't be grateful enough to Drescal for removing Gregory. I know it was Drescal now, because he's just snuck back into the room and is inching closer to us. Lucifer's surprised look lands on his twin, former Heaven's Guardian, now sporting a pair of black wings and a surly look.

"But you," he says, his eyes zeroing back in on me. He glides forward. I don't move a muscle. "I have waited for you for an awfully long time, girl. What is your name?"

Girl? Girl? Who the fuck does this dick think he is?

"Annabelle," I grit out. "*The Devil*, at your service."

"Hm," he murmurs. "We'll see about that."

I open my mouth to blast him to the Wastelands and back, but at my dad's slight shake of his head, I slam it shut again. Why? Because I want to smash his face in instead. I clench my fists, ready to Shift for the fight of my life, when he speaks again and gives me pause.

"The Anti-Christ. You are perfection." He takes my hand and kisses my palm lightly.

Killian's hand shoots out and grips my elbow so tightly, he hits the nerve in it, making me squirm.

"We have much to discuss," Lucifer says. "Come."

His fingers tighten on my hand, and in the split second before he flames out with me, Xavi grabs onto the belt hook of my jeans. Wherever Lucifer is taking me, War and Pestilence have followed.

As I look around at the previously undiscovered cavern, deep in the bowels of Hell, I'm suddenly glad to have them at my side.

CHAPTER 32

Aleister

"WHERE HAS SHE GONE?" Axelle shrieks in a voice so loud, I wince. "Where the fuck is she?"

"We'll find her," the former Devil says to his wife, crushing her to him in a kiss so erotic, everyone looks away.

Except me. I'm still staring at him, a bit shocked that he is here again when he was supposed to be dead. I knew it, but I don't think it processed until just now.

"Find her," Axelle shouts, pulling away from Luc. The former Hell Queen is making the ground shake underneath us in her agitation and fury.

"I can't sense her," Shax says.

"He'll have cloaked her," Luc says and then stumbles back as Drescal swoops over to him, giving him a manly embrace, where they bang each other on the back.

"It's good to see you, old friend," Drescal says.

"You too," Luc says with a smirk. "I see you got your wish?"

"I did," he nods, returning the grin.

I'm slightly envious. Not of Luc but of Drescal. They are clearly close. I wish that I had been. Annabelle worships her dad, that much is clear. I want him to accept me.

"Killian and Xavier are with her," Luc says, turning back to Axelle. "She will be safe."

"She can kick Lucifer's ass herself," I state, defending her.

Luc's sparkling blue eyes land on me. "Aleister," he says. "You know my daughter?"

"Uhm," Axelle murmurs. "All of these males are hers," she adds quietly.

Luc's eyes harden as he turns back to her. "She followed you?"

Axelle nods.

"Fuck's sake, woman. I gave you one job!" he snaps. "I told you to get her hooked up with Drescal. That did not include all of these other fuckers."

Axelle presses her lips together, trying not to smile under the circumstances.

"She is her own being, dear. There was fuck all I could do about this."

He looks like he is about to shoot through the roof in rage, but then he sighs and shakes his head.

"I will go and find her," he says. "You," he says to me. "You are loyal, at least you have that going for you. You will come with me. The rest of you scatter. Scour Hell until you find her."

I nod.

He grabs my arm, but then Axelle makes a muffled noise and clutches her stomach.

Evan is at her side in a heartbeat. "Is everything okay?" he asks.

"Mm-hm," she mutters, but her face tells a different story.

"Go with them," I say to Luc. "We've got this. We will find Annabelle, I promise you that."

His eyes bore into mine. "Are you willing to bet your life on it?" he asks.

"Yes," I state, knowing that even if we don't find Annabelle or Lucifer has hurt her, my life will be over anyway.

"Go," Drescal says.

After another pause, he nods. "Fine. I will hold every single one of you responsible if he hurts even a hair on her head."

"No!" Axelle says, panting. "Go with them."

"Axelle, we've got this," I say quietly.

Her panicked look meets mine, but I give her a reassuring smile.

I feel she is about to protest further, but a rush of blood floods down her legs, causing us all to take a giant step back and avert our eyes.

"Go!" Drescal says and they don't need telling again.

"Uhm," Devlin says, finally coming out of his stupor. "What did you do with Gregory?"

"I put him in Annabelle's room with Sid. He's awake by the way. Musmortus is guarding the door."

"From the inside?" I venture with a frown.

Drescal gives me a withering glare. "No, the outside. Not that it makes much difference. If she wanted in, she'd get in."

Elijah snorts his agreement, but then sobers quickly. "We need to find Anna."

"I'm guessing he'd have taken her to the caverns," Shax says, sidling forward to our group. "However, Belle and I have barely discovered a *fraction* of what is down there. It could literally take us weeks to find them."

"Great," I mutter, but then pull it together. "I know that I can't get to the caverns. Anyone else?"

Everyone shakes their head, so we look at Shax. He holds his hands out grimly. "I don't know how many I can take at a time, and I'm held responsible for what happens when we get down there. You can't access it for a reason."

I grip his right hand as Elijah firmly takes hold of his left. If I didn't know better, I'd say I saw a spark light up as their palms touched.

I frown and shake my head. "Let's go."

"I'll be back for you two, if you're not scared," Shax taunts Devlin and Drescal seeing as they were a bit slower to reach out.

"Fuck you, mate," Devlin snarls. "Those two were closer."

"Agreed," Drescal growls, going a bit alpha on our asses. It's quite attractive to see his smooth, suave self get a bit riled up.

Shax sneers at them and then with a flap of his wings, we are deep underground, near the center of Hell.

Shax shakes us off him the second we land and disappears, not waiting to see if we burn up and get eradicated for entering the über un-consecrated ground.

We both stand there, frozen in place, but when, after a few seconds, we *don't* set on fire, we both relax a bit.

I feel the pure evil of this place and even Elijah is looking a little less than confident as we wait for Shax to return.

He does, with Devlin and Drescal, and lets them go as quickly as he did us.

He gives us all a speculative look, as if expecting us to start smoldering. I can't help but feel that he is disappointed when we don't.

"What now?" I ask. "We don't have the time to wander around and around looking for her. You must know something?" I look at Shax with slight desperation. The longer we are down here, the more it is affecting me. I think it is getting to the other males as well. They all look as uncomfortable as I feel. Every breath I take, sears my lungs a little bit more.

"The only place that I can think of is the sacrificial chamber. But who knows if they are in there and if there is more than one?"

"It's a start," Elijah growls. "Go back and get Mouse. Bring her here. She will find her Mistress, or at least have a better chance than we do."

Shax grits his teeth, annoyed to be ordered about. "I'll take you to the chamber first. If they aren't there, I'll go back," he states and once again holds his hands out. Devlin and Drescal, unsurprisingly, reach him first this time.

"Wait!" I say. "You can't just burst in unprepared. What if they are there?"

"Then Shax will have to be quick bringing you two losers, won't he?" Devlin answers and with a snort, Shax transports them out.

"This is a disaster," I mutter.

"No shit," Elijah mutters back.

Shax returns. "They aren't there. I'll take you two and go back for Mouse," he says resigned. He knows he has to get on board with all of us helping Annabelle.

"Thanks," I say and off we go to join the other two.

I draw in a deep breath and then look sharply to the side.

"What?" Elijah pounces like a Hound scenting blood.

"The evil is greater over on that side of the chamber," I say, using my Gargoyle senses to track it.

"Oh?" Devlin mutters, giving me a curious look.

I roll my eyes at him. "Gargoyles are used to protect the Ruler of Hell from all manner of, well, for lack of a better word, *evil* against them. We can sense and track evil in a greater form. This way," I say decisively and march off. I don't care if they believe me or follow me, but I'm going.

As it happens, they all scramble to catch up, even Shax.

"So, we don't need Mouse?"

"Not yet," I mutter and stop at the fork on the far side of

the chamber. I close my eyes and concentrate on the evil emanating out of the tunnels.

"Left," I mutter and enter the tunnel. It is dark and not just from a lack of light.

"Here," Shax says and flicks his palm out, a fireball hovering over it to guide the way.

I glance at it and he knows what I'm thinking. "Can't kill you with it," he informs me. "It's light, that's all."

I nod grimly, knowing that I have to trust him. We are all in this together.

I'm cautious though. After my near-death experience at the hands of Darius and his briar poison darts, I can't help but be a bit skittish. I don't fear death. I never have. It is inevitable in my line of work, not to mention there will always be someone more powerful who takes offense at your plain face if not something worse. My predecessor died because Leviathan wanted *me* as Master Gargoyle. Okay, so it did kind of diminish the honor when I found out, but I have proven myself time and again to two rulers of Hell. No, what I fear is losing Annabelle. The worry that I have for her is clawing at me. It has taken me in its grip, and I can't shake it off. I'm glad we are acting. I'm glad that *I* am able to find her down here. She is my everything. From the first time I kneeled before her and accused her of playing a dark and dangerous game, she grabbed my heart and hasn't let go. I don't care that I have to share her. All I care about is that she wants me. I know that she loves me, even though she won't say it. Her actions when I was dying spoke much, *much* louder and I don't need to hear the three words. I know how she feels and it's enough. I saw her fear of losing me and her love swimming in those amazing green eyes and that's all I need.

We wind our way through an absolute maze of tunnels, caverns, and caves as the time ticks away.

Eventually I sense her.

I stop and hold my hand up. All of the men have been silent while we searched. I turn to them and whisper. "In there," I point to a large maw in the black rock on the opposite side of the small cave we are in. "We need a plan."

"I'll go first," Shax says. "If she's Shifted, then none of you will stand a chance."

I open my mouth to counteract his plan. What the Hell are we supposed to do while he goes off playing hero? Stand here like a bunch of fuckwits?

"I don't fucking think so," Elijah snarls and before any of us can stop him, he is racing towards the cavern opening, seconds away from Shifting.

"Wait!" I hiss at him. "Elijah!"

CHAPTER 33

Annabelle

"You have got some nerve, you know that?" I say to Lucifer. "You don't get to come here and tell me what to do."

"But I do, girl. Hell is *mine*. It always was and always will be," he replies, his eyes sparking up with flames.

It doesn't deter me. *I* am the Devil now. He might have his powers, some, or all, it makes no difference. I *know* that I have a full working set, Leviathan will attest to that.

"Nope, Hell is *mine*. You aren't even the *former* ruler. You are so far in the past now, no one cares about you anymore. Not even your little bitch, Leviathan. She is currently enduring her own personal Hell and will do so for all eternity for fucking with what is mine. Try it, Great-Gramps and you will see how wrathful I can be."

My hands are on my hips, but Killian and Xavier haven't taken their hands off me yet. I try to shake them off, but they aren't budging.

I hear a scuffle somewhere behind me and know that Killian did as well when he stiffens even more. I swear to myself, if my other males come charging in to rescue me, Lucifer's won't be the only ass I'll kick.

Lucifer's eyes return to normal and he gives me a big beam. "Oh, you are so precious. You are exactly how I hoped my son would be. It's unfortunate that firstly, you are a female and secondly, you aren't my own. That, however, makes no difference in the grand plan. You *will* walk the Earth and start the Apocalypse. You two," he indicates War and Pestilence, "will do your fucking jobs with the others and end the World. I *want those souls.*"

His whole nicey-nice presence deteriorates with those three words. He is starting to Shift and I'm pretty sure my other males are now planning to storm the cavern. They will die. Without a doubt. I won't be able to save them all.

Killian pulls me back by my hand. "Don't start this fight on his terms," he mutters to me.

"Erm, have no choice," I mutter back. I prepare to Shift and ready myself for the fight of my life.

"No!" Killian shouts and I look over my shoulder to see Elijah, in Hellhound form, charge into the cavern, snarling and fueled with rage.

But it's too late, Lucifer has finished his Shift, and is towering over us in his full Devil form. I shriek as I speed up my own Shift and my Devil form rips through me. I fire off a ball of Hellfire, so large it would eradicate an entire army of regular Demons but Lucifer swats it away and fires off a similar ball in my direction.

I hold my hand out, palm outwards and deflect it, sending it flying straight back to him.

I cast a glance at Elijah, thinking he must've fried up to a crisp by now, but I'm shocked to see him still alive and pouncing at Lucifer, all three of his mouths wide open to chomp down on some Devil's ass.

"Fuck!" I scream, my throat tearing in two from the sound.

Xavier is firing bolts of ice at her creator, while Killian is channeling as much of his energy into me as he can. It nearly knocks me off my fucking feet. He has *juice*. Mingled with mine, it is creating a power inside of me that I know I'm going to crave once this is done.

"Elijah," I growl, the only sound I can make now with my bleeding throat.

"He's fine," Killian says steadily. "Use what I'm giving you."

I nod and accept it. I trust him. It's a new fucking concept for me. But these are exceptional circumstances.

Lucifer is struggling with Elijah, who hasn't released him from his jaws even a tiny bit, despite having the fires of Hell singe his fur.

It makes my heart thump.

The fear that shoots through me at the thought of losing my Hellhound, makes me focus and I hold my hand up towards Killian, forming a fireball the size of Mouse. It grows and grows as Killian channels more power into me.

"Xavi," I mutter, "get Elijah to move."

I know I'm ready for this. I was ready to end this before Killian suped up my power. Sure, Lucifer and I probably would have battled it out for a lot longer as we'd have been evenly matched, but this is different. I can feel it.

With a loud howl, Elijah releases Lucifer and I fling the fireball at the first ruler of Hell. It seems to fly over to him in slow motion as I see and process him creating his own fireball and preparing to throw it at Elijah. Just as he is about to release it, my fireball hits him in the chest, and he stumbles back. His fireball leaves his hand, but doesn't hit his mark square on.

"Elijah!" I rasp and lunge forward.

He was still hit, grazed down his right flank, knocking him off his feet and forcing him to Shift back to his human form.

"Fuck," I grate out.

I step forward to go to him, but Killian's, "No!" stops me. "Finish this!" he urges, bringing my focus back to Lucifer. I turn back to face him, my lungs searing every time I breathe in.

I got him good, but not good enough. He is recovering from the hit. "I'm going to need a bigger ball," I whisper, swallowing blood from my torn throat.

I look back at Killian and shake my head. He must see something in my Devil's goat eyes as he nods grimly and says, "Lock him in."

He pulls back his magick and spins to scoop Elijah up and throw him over his shoulder. He shouts to Xavi and she runs, knowing that she needs to get out of my way.

I put my hands together and draw on the reserve of magick that runs so deep inside me, I can feel it in the pit of my stomach. The darkness washes over me. My rational thought leaves and the need to destroy rears up. I have dug as deep as I did with Leviathan and the weird thing is, I suddenly know that this isn't it. There is more, I just need to access it.

I twist my hands and pull them apart, growing the Hellfire between my palms. I don't give Lucifer a chance to fully get over the last one. I just throw it at him, hitting him in the face and then I run, diving through the hole in the wall that leads out of the cavern and into a smaller cave, Shifting at the same time so that I don't kill my males.

I land on my back with a painful crunch, but throw my hands up and send a wave of power towards the cavern entrance just as Lucifer lunges for it.

I stifle my shriek as the males all dive for cover, hiding

their eyes so they don't accidentally gaze upon him and end their Demonic lives.

The magick bounces visibly as Lucifer hits it, snarling and drooling like the savage beast he is. With me on the floor on my back and in human form, he appears so much bigger now as I look up at him.

"Hold, you fucker," I mutter to the forcefield that is locking him in. "Just hold until I figure this out."

It appears to do as I beseech, even with Lucifer pounding on it with his gigantic fists and raking his sword-like talons down it.

"Elijah," I pant and crawl over to him, where Killian has placed him on the ground.

I stifle my noise of shock. He is bleeding profusely; the entire right side of his torso is hanging off. Normally this wouldn't affect me, but seeing one of my lovers like this, makes me want to vomit.

"My love," I whisper to him, taking his face in my hands.

He grunts and lets out a strangled laugh. "It's more than I expected," he gasps, his breathing labored.

"Fuck you," I hold back the sob that threatens to come out. "Die and I will fucking kill you."

Aleister drops to his knees next to me and I look at him. "Let's get him back to the residence," he says quietly.

Killian wordlessly picks him up and vanishes with him, Shax takes Aleister and Drescal, which leaves Xavi and Devlin.

"Take him, please," I say to Xavi.

"Belle," she says, her voice tight. "Do not do anything stupid. Come back with us and we will figure this out together."

She grabs my hand.

I look at Lucifer still growling and lashing out at the

forcefield. That thing isn't going to hold forever. If he gets out, all bets are off. I have to finish this.

"Annie," Devlin says, taking my other hand. "We will finish this, once we've fixed Elijah."

I don't answer.

I don't resist when I feel Xavi's icy breeze wash over me.

"I can't do this again," I say stiffly when we land in Elijah's bedroom at the residence, with everyone surrounding him, including Gregory and Sid.

I give Xavi a panicked look. "I can't do this again," I repeat and back out, pulling a cloak of disinterest over me to protect myself from the pain. I turn around and stalk to my bedroom, slamming the door shut behind me.

CHAPTER 34

Killian

I WATCH as Annabelle leaves the room. I want to go to her and drag her back, but she needs a minute. Her stricken expression when she looked at Elijah hurts me. She is in so much pain, but also in denial. Her focus will only be on eradicating Lucifer once and for all.

"You need to mix your blood with Annabelle's," I say to Shax. He looks at me with a puzzled frown.

"Long story, it healed Aleister. It has to work on this as well," I say shortly. I have to push my own pain aside and deal with this.

"I'll go to Belle," he says quietly, accepting what I've said.

"No, I'll go," Gregory says. "She is hurting, she has distanced herself. I will get this done quicker."

Shax nods briefly and Gregory disappears through the door.

"Hang on," I whisper to Elijah, squeezing his hand.

He grunts and closes his eyes. He is still breathing though, so I take the opportunity to grab Devlin by the arm and haul him to the other side of the room.

"Start speaking," I state.

He looks back at me, cocky as ever. "What do you want me to say?"

"I know that you know more than you're letting on about what you read in the codex. It wasn't just some reference to the number of the beast. What. Was. It?" I grit out.

He debates with himself for a second. "Okay, mate. You got me. I read several pages of the codex that night before Annabelle woke up, and I remember most of it."

"I'm only interested in the bit we discussed," I spit out, getting seriously annoyed with this little shit. Fucking Necros and their games.

"Fine," he huffs. "But you didn't hear it from me. I'm not even supposed to be able to see the damned thing, never mind be able to *read* it."

"I'm aware," I snarl. It is a mystery beyond aggravating how he has managed what Demons twice as powerful can't.

"From the number of the beast, a new Hell will rise," he quotes.

My heart skips a beat. I didn't think it was possible. I did not think it was something that *could* happen, never mind be something that I *want* so desperately it makes me long to go to her and tell her.

But I can't.

There is no way she will accept it. She will reject the news and it will hurt me because she doesn't love me. She doesn't love any of us.

I have never loved before, but I know that I love the Demon Queen. It is fierce, full of passion and lust, tinged with a darkness that makes me sweat with the sheer rapture of it. I adore her. I respect her, even though I love challenging her and I don't want to exist without her.

To me, that is love. If I'm wrong, then someone will have to explain it to me, but I don't think that I am.

"Killian," Devlin says, snapping his fingers in front of my face. "Does it mean something to you?"

"No," I state and turn away from him.

"Then what the fuck was all of this about?" he complains as I walk away.

I ignore him. I have to think. The codex is an unusual beast. Don't make the mistake of thinking it isn't sentient. It changes its words to suit and more than once, Lucifer found himself struggling to keep up with it, as well as his son and grandson. But I'm as certain as I can be about the accuracy of this revelation.

Annabelle is pregnant with my child.

I *felt* a new power simmering under her surface when I gave her mine. I hadn't been at all sure that she would be able to accept my power and use it. I think she only could because of the child. The essence latched on it and drew it in, handing it off to its mother to use.

I reach Elijah's side at the same time that Annabelle and Gregory re-enter the room.

I try not to gaze into her eyes because I know that if I do, I will spill the truth to her and set myself up for a kick in the balls that will hurt me for an exceptionally long time. She needs to come to this realization herself and process it in her own time before she tells anyone else. I know this much about her.

"How do we know this will even work?" she mutters, trying not to look at Elijah.

"You have to try," I say softly.

Her eyes meet mine and I can see the sheen of unshed tears in her eyes. I reach out to her and take her hand, lacing our fingers together. She nods briefly, but she doesn't look at Elijah. She just holds her hand out to Shax. He slashes her palm and then his own, even though I saw it was already wounded. He holds her hand tightly and squeezes. They drop the blood into Elijah's wound, causing him to groan and buck with pain as it hisses and sizzles.

We all wait to see if he will come to like Aleister did, but after a long time nothing happens.

"Shax, cauterize the wound with just your blood," I say quietly.

He gives me a surprised look. It will cause Elijah more pain than he is currently enduring, but it will buy him some time.

"Do it," Annabelle says quietly.

Shax hesitates for only a second before he pulls his hand away from Annabelle's and reopens the closed wound on one palm and then cuts open the other one. He places his hands over Elijah and the blood drops into the wound.

Elijah's scream of pain makes Annabelle gag and she turns towards me, pressing her face into my chest so she doesn't have to see it. I wrap my arms around her.

"Enough," I say to Shax and he shoots me a grateful look. I'd heard that he rather enjoys torturing Demons this way, but I guess when the Demon in question is involved with his sister, it's a different story.

"He's stopped bleeding," I tell Annabelle.

She lets out the breath she'd been holding. "I'm going to look in the codex for a way to kill Lucifer and fix *this*," she states and once again walks out. Her hurt fills my senses, but I don't go with her. She needs to be alone. She will call us when she has something to say.

I just hope that is sooner rather than later.

CHAPTER 35

Elijah

I TRY NOT to groan from the searing agony that is coursing through my body with each breath I take. Everyone is standing over me, except Xavier. More importantly, except Annabelle. It hurts worse that she left me. But I get it. She is going through the fear of losing someone again. If she was here, though, I could tell her that she isn't going to lose me. Not a fucking chance am I exiting this world without two things. One, that I get to tell her that I love her and two, I need her to say it back. I need to hear those words come out of her perfect, dirty mouth and see her be vulnerable for just a second.

In fact, I want it right now.

I do emit a groan as I struggle to sit up and swing my legs over the side of the bed.

"Whoa," Shax says and grabs my shoulders. "Where do you think you're going, big boy?"

I sneer at him. If I wasn't about to get up off my sorry ass to tell his sister that I love her, I would show him how big I am. Shady fucker. I saw that box; I know what he's into.

"I'm not lying around on this bed while Annabelle needs help," I state. "Get out of my way."

"E," Killian says. "You haven't healed. We've patched you up, that's it."

"I know," I growl. "I've stopped bleeding. I will heal on my own now."

"Erm, I have a question," Devlin asks, sidling a bit closer, his eyes blazing into mine with curiosity. "How the actual fuck did you do that?"

"Do what?" I ask just to piss him off. I enjoy the flash of black I see in his bright blue eyes when he gets mad or turned on. It's sexy as fuck.

There it is.

I smirk at him.

He grits his teeth. "You survived not only seeing Annabelle in her Devil form, but Lucifer as well. How? And don't give us some bullshit answer. Truth, Elijah."

I rub my hand over my face and wince as the action pulls on my wound. "I drank her blood," I state eventually. "It made me a part of her, able to see her in all her forms and help her."

I give the rest of them a challenging stare, but Killian's intense gaze bores into my head and I turn to look at him as Shax steps back a fraction, folding his arms over his chest.

"You drank her blood?" Drescal asks. "When? How? Does she know?"

"Yes, the other day when we were fucking, I bit her and yes she does. Although, I don't think she gets the implications of the act."

"You drank her blood?" Killian asks quietly, almost possessively.

"You were there," I say to him. "You saw it."

"I saw you *bite* her," he growls.

"What did you think I was doing while I was biting her? Apart from fucking her, that is," I ask.

"You are a first-class asshole, you know that," he snarls. "There is no way she knows it was her blood that made you semi-invincible."

"Semi?" I scoff. "I survived, didn't I?"

"Barely," he sneers at me.

I grit my teeth at him. He is seriously pissed off and it's making him mean. It wouldn't usually bother me, but I'm feeling a bit delicate right now.

I glance at Sid. He has stuffed himself into the corner of the room. I totally get why he is so traumatized. Being burned by Hellfire is not fun. I tear my gaze away from him and focus on Killian again.

"This is the key to helping her," he says after a beat.

"Yep," I agree. "I had no idea about it at the time. I do now. I *know* that's why I survived seeing them."

"We need to go to Annabelle now," Killian says.

"Wait," Devlin says, holding up his hand. "This still doesn't really help. All it will do is give Lucifer more of us to pick off."

"That's not very supportive," I inform him and stand up. My legs shake and my knees almost buckle, but I grimace and suck it up. I wrap my left arm over my body and hold my right side as I take a step forward.

"Hey!" he says sharply, drawing my focus back to him and his dark blue eyes. "I'm her biggest supporter. But you have to admit that without a plan to get rid of Lucifer, us being there isn't going to help."

"Yes, it will," Killian says.

I give him a grateful smile for backing me up, but he ignores it, still pissed off with me.

"We can find a way to help her. She said she needed a

bigger ball. We are going to give her one," he says cryptically and stalks off, leaving me to make my own way across the room before Shax takes pity on me and grabs my elbow.

"Thanks," I mutter.

"You should be in bed," he mutters back. "I stuck you back together, but you don't seem to be healing."

"I will," I say. "I can already feel it. Annabelle's blood won't let me die."

He gives me a searching look, but stays silent as he helps me follow Killian, and everyone else troops out behind us.

Killian is already standing in her room when we arrive, looking even more annoyed. "She isn't here," he states. "If she's gone back…"

"She hasn't," Xavi says, appearing behind us in a flurry of icy smoke. "She is with her parents. Shax, you should go."

He lets go of me instantly and disappears.

"Is Axelle okay?" Drescal asks.

Xavi shakes her head. "Not good," she says. "Luc is about to raze Hell to the ground unless Annabelle can help."

"How?" I ask quietly.

"I didn't get much, but something to do with ripping the child out. They're combining their power or something."

"Precisely what *we* need to do," Killian says. He points to the corner where an empty pedestal sits. "Devlin," he snaps. "Go find something."

"Excuse me?" he asks. "How the fuck am I supposed to find something in there?"

"In what?" I ask. I give up my fight to stay on my feet and sit heavily on the bed.

"The codex," Killian says. "Our little Necro here can see it and read it for some reason unbeknownst to me."

"Gee, thanks," Devlin mutters as the rest of us gape at him.

No one says a word though, as he hesitantly edges

towards the plinth. He holds his hands up at some force the rest of us can't see and then he slips around the pedestal, placing his hands on either side of it.

After a few minutes of watching him turn invisible pages, I flop back to the bed. Killian sits next to me and takes my hand.

"Did you fuck her in your Hellhound form?" he asks me quietly.

"Yes," I answer. "Did you fuck her in your Horseman form?"

"Yes," he replies, giving me a soft smirk.

I chuckle. "I wish I could've seen that."

"Same. I want to. I want to watch you be with her that way."

"Ask her," I whisper now running out of steam. It hurts to do everything, even lie still.

"Die and *I* will kill you," he whispers back, stroking my face.

I snort and then cough, wincing at the same time. I've never felt such pain before. I should be healing by now. I won't say that I'm worried, because, fuck that. *But* marginally concerned, maybe. I feel my eyes close and then I'm jolted awake by the return of Annabelle, her face a mix of delight and fury.

CHAPTER 36

Annabelle

"WHAT THE FUCK do you think you are doing?" I spit out, glaring at Devlin pawing through the codex. "How, even?"

He shrugs. "Not sure how but trying to help. I can see it, read it."

"Since when?" I ask with narrowed eyes.

"Since always," he replies cautiously.

"Oh, really?" I drawl, hands on my hips. Little fucking sneak. Not to mention, how can he do this? The codex is for the Devil's eyes only. Not even my mother can read it. Nor Shax, that I know of.

I flick my gaze to him as he appears next me.

"What?" he asks.

"Nothing," I mutter.

"How's your mother?" Killian asks, coming to me and giving me a soft kiss on my head.

"Fine," I breathe out with a smile. "Happy baby boy, also doing well."

"Good," he says and squeezes my shoulder. Then, dropping his hand, he brushes it over my stomach before it falls to his side.

"So, Devlin. Bypassing the fact that you can see and read the codex, have you found anything?" I ask

He shakes his head. "I don't even know what I'm looking for," he says with a sigh.

"A way to give her a bigger ball," Killian says, glaring at him.

"Easy for you to say," he grouses. "Do you know how cryptic this fucker is? It's garbled."

"Maybe because you aren't supposed to be reading it," I point out and stalk over, pushing him out of the way.

"Point taken," he murmurs and backs off.

I glare at the page in front of me.

After a minute, I sigh. Devlin is right. It's a mess of words. *Meht evol* keeps popping out of the swarm of words that are making me go dizzy.

"What the fuck does *meht evol* mean?" I ask, banging my hand on the codex.

"Hmm?" Killian asks. He is sitting next to Elijah on the bed again.

"Is he okay?" I ask quietly, pushing the hurt away from seeing him this way.

"*He* is fine," Elijah says, sitting up and going pale at the same time.

I bite my lip. Well, 'A' for effort, but a massive fail at being okay.

I stare at him, having nothing to say, or at least, nothing that will come out. I want to say lots of things, but the words can't get past my throat.

I look back at the codex.

Xavi steps up to the pedestal with a mirror in her hand. I

peer at it and fix my hair, puckering up and thinking I look fab.

She giggles at me. "Hold the book up," she says. "Standard Demonic practice."

"Oh," I say with a snort.

"Not that you don't look amazing," she adds and blows me a kiss.

I preen and grab the book, turning it around.

"Uhm," I say as the words jump out at me and are all over the two pages reflected in the mirror. I slam the book back down and look at Xavi.

"What did it say?" Gregory asks.

I look up at him and press my lips together.

Sid comes a bit closer and I smile at him. I hold my hand out and he takes it. "Glad you're okay," I murmur.

"Thank you for what you did," he mutters and kisses my hand gently before he lets it go. "You need to say it. To all of them."

"Why?" I croak out, ignoring everyone else.

"The codex wants you to," he says simply and then backs away.

"What did it say?" Gregory asks again.

I exchange a look with Xavi, and she nods her head briefly.

"You can say it, it won't kill you," she says with a small smile.

She moves out of the way so that I can take in all of them. I take a deep breath and let it out. I focus not on any one of them, but on the window that looks out over the sin bin. "It says *love them*. Over and over again."

Silence.

"And?" Drescal presses after an uncomfortable moment.

"And nothing. That's it," I say, feeling very uncomfortable. I could say the words to Sid because he needed to hear them from me to help him heal. He needed to know that what he gave me was the ability to love him and protect him.

"Just say it," Xavi says. "I know you feel it. Just say it."

I glare at her. Shit-stirrer.

"Fine," I huff out. "I love you all, okay. There I've said it."

"Wow," Drescal snickers. "Exactly how I wanted to hear it from your lips."

I give him a death stare, but he swoops in to kiss me, pushing his tongue into my mouth as his arms go around me.

"I love you, Anna," he says, pulling away. "However you say it, it doesn't matter, as long as you feel the same."

I smile at him.

He steps to the side and I look at each of them in turn. Then, I look back at the codex and mumble. "I love you all, very much. The words don't come easy and I hadn't wanted to single any of you out to say it first." I ignore the fact that I've already done that. "So, here we are, all together."

"All together," Killian says, standing up and coming over to me. "That's what we are now, Annabelle, together. All of us. We will be with you always and there isn't a single thing that you can't ask of us. We will always be here for you."

"Agreed," Devlin says.

I then look up and smile, my confidence returning. Elijah stands up and walks over to me slowly. He takes my hand.

"I love you, Annabelle."

I feel a bit shy all of a sudden and hope that all of this touchy-feely bullshit is over soon.

"How do you feel?" I ask him and prod him in his side.

He winces fiercely, but gives me a smile. "Just fine," he grits out.

"Pah," I scoff gently. "Elijah, how did you..."

"He drank your blood, that's how!" Devlin interjects.

I frown at Elijah. "What? How did you know it would make you able to see me?"

"I didn't," he responds grimly. "I drank your blood when I bit you the other day. The taste of it…I couldn't stop myself. I didn't even think about it until I pounced on Lucifer and then it all just clicked."

"Oh," I say a bit taken aback. "But this is good, in a way. Obviously, we don't want this getting out…"

"Obviously," Killian interrupts me, "but it means they can help you as well. If everyone drinks your blood, then they will be able to face down Lucifer, while we combine our power with yours. You just need to find a spell in there to do it." He points to the codex.

"Easy as that," I murmur and flip the upside-down codex over and rifle through the pages. "What did me telling you all I love you have to do with anything?" I muse while I seek whatever the fuck I'm supposed to be looking for.

"It opened up your heart to accept the help we can offer you," Drescal says quietly.

I glance up and give him a quick smile.

I suppose I don't *have* to do everything myself, but I like having the burden on my shoulders. It gives me a purpose. If I contracted everything out, what use would I be? None at all, really.

Everyone goes quiet as I continue to turn the pages and then I see something.

"A spell!" I shout out, making everyone jump. "It's a circle. We are already a circle, so this should be a piece of cake. It will require all of you, all of those that I love. Sorry, Gregory, but that includes you. You will be protected by my blood…"

"*And* by us," Killian interrupts me. "No one falls, I can promise you that."

I give him a quick nod and focus on Gregory. He doesn't look anything except valiant. Oh, how I do love him. So accepting, so bold and brave. He is completely out of his depth and yet he does this…for me.

He bobs his head, a grim look on his face and then I get to work, ordering everyone about to bring me what I need to complete our circle and boost my power with the one thing that I seriously didn't think would be of *any* use down in Hell.

Love.

CHAPTER 37

Shax

"Do you need me for a while?" I ask Belle. "There's something I have to sort out."

"Oh, with your little pet?" she asks with more than a bit of snark.

"Yes," I state and glare at her.

"Fine, go, but there is something that I need from you. Let's walk." She takes me by the arm and leads me out into the hallway, closing the bedroom door behind her. We stop outside of my bedroom door. "That dagger of yours, the one that you carry everywhere, how come it hurts you but not me?"

"A long story that you don't need to know about," I say.

"Stop being cagey, for once, Shax. Tell me," she demands.

"Because I don't want to hurt you when I cut myself," I snap at her, giving her a look that speaks volumes.

"What?" she asks quietly. "Why would you do that?"

"Doesn't matter. I don't feel the urge anymore."

"Shax..."

"Look, I don't want to talk about it and I really do need to sort something out now."

"I need it," she says, thankfully dropping the topic of my self harm, but it's not forgotten. Oh no, her face tells me that.

"What for?" I ask warily.

"Lucifer will still be in his Devil form without a doubt when we go back down there. I need him in human form. I think that dagger with your blood on it, piercing his heart will force him to Shift."

"How so?" I ask, intrigued.

"It is clearly imbued with heavy dark magick, plus your blood…just call it a hunch."

"I'll bring it," I say and then push open my bedroom door to see Shadow curled up on my bed fast asleep.

I shut the door quietly.

"Hey," I say as she wakes up with a start. "Just me."

"Shax," she says and rubs her eyes. "About Bannister, I don't want it. I swear to you…"

"I know," I say with a sigh. "I believe you. It just hurts that this is coming between us. I'd hoped we were past all of the drama."

"Same," she says, chewing her lip. "I've come to a decision," she blurts out after a beat.

I wait for her to gather her thoughts. She nervously wrings her hands and then climbs off the bed to pace. My heart is thumping in my chest. I have absolutely no clue what she is going to say or do. She is the hardest female to read, ever.

"I'm going to tell the Griffins, *show* the Griffins, what I am," she says eventually. "Tell them that we are in love and that I'm going to spend most of my time in human form to be with you."

I just stare at her in shock.

"If you'll have me," she says quietly, looking down. "I

know I'm not the easiest female to be with. I'm selfish and inconsiderate sometimes, but it's just that I don't really know how else to be. If you could take the time to show me…"

I don't let her finish. I fling myself at her, sweeping her off her feet and kissing her deeply, pouring every ounce of love I have for her into it.

She returns it just as forcefully, leaving me breathless and wishing that we could do this forever. Unfortunately, there will be no us, no Hell, no *anything* if Lucifer gets out of the cavern before Belle gets to him with the spell she is concocting.

I pull away from her, cupping her face and smiling at her.

"I have some family business that needs taking care of urgently," I whisper to her. "I will be back as soon as I can."

"Can I come with you?" she asks hopefully.

I kiss her softly, wishing she could, but I won't risk her. Not a chance. "No, love. This is dangerous and I don't want you getting hurt."

"Dangerous?" she asks full of concern. "Will you be okay?"

"I'll be fine. We all will when this is over with."

She nods slowly as I let go. "Please come back to me, Shax," she says.

I give her a brief nod and a smile, then I duck back out of the bedroom, elated that something finally went my way. I curse myself as I realize that I've probably just jinxed it, but come to a halt at Belle's door, intrigued as to the massive argument going on between Drescal and some other fucker who has turned up, which makes a lot of sense when he suddenly turns around.

"Shax, my old pal," Salax says, giving me a punch on the arm. "Long time. So, hear I'm needed for an ass kicking?"

I groan. This isn't going to go well. Drescal and Salax do not get on. It's unsurprising. Drescal is an Incubus and Salax is a Dark Cupid. He makes his living infecting humans with lust, making Drescal's job of seducing them practically redundant.

This is going to be a disaster. I can just see it.

Unfortunately, Salax seems to have caught Annabelle's attention in a big way with his cute face and blond hair. She is gazing at him with a look that has Killian in his 'miserable cunt' mode.

"Yep, a fucking disaster," I mutter and enter the room, closing the door behind me.

CHAPTER 38

Annabelle

I BLINK at the Dark Cupid that has fallen in my lap. Figuratively speaking. Although I wouldn't say no to a literal falling either. He is *hot*, in a seriously cute way. It's the combination that has piqued my interest. Coupled with the fact that he spreads my favorite Deadly Sin around, makes him very enticing indeed.

I get that Drescal doesn't like him. It must be difficult to do your job when you have someone fucking it up for you on a daily basis. *Ex* job.

"So, Salax, is it?" I ask. "You are our special ingredient for a very special spell."

His blue eyes focus on me, giving me a sexy once-over that Killian does not appreciate in the slightest.

"Am I now?" Salax asks huskily. "How can I help, my Queen?"

"You can keep your eyes on her face, you fucking prick," Drescal snarls at him.

"But her rack is amazing, it was made to be looked at," Salax replies with a cheeky smirk.

"You are looking for an arse-kicking, mate." Devlin gets in on the growling.

"Feel free to keep looking," I say, pissing the males off even further. Xavi, on the other hand, is howling with laughter at this. "But we do have a pressing matter to attend to."

"Yes," Killian states loudly, drawing the attention to him. "We need to get this done, Annabelle, so if you would please move this along."

"Yes, sir," I mutter, earning a vicious look from my sweet War. "Shax, the dagger please." I hold my hand out for it.

He slaps it against my palm, giving me a look that screams at me to stop playing a dangerous game, but he doesn't get to dictate to me. If I want to flirt with the Dark Cupid, then I will.

I move back behind the plinth and move the codex. It hovers in midair next to me and I summon up a big copper bowl. I slash my wrist with a hiss and bleed into the bowl, letting enough pour in to half fill it. I give the dagger back to Shax which he shoves in the back of his jeans.

"Salax, this is where you come in," I murmur.

"How so?" he asks, looking intrigued.

"I need you to amp up this spell with love."

"Uhm, sorry, sweetheart, I deal with lust. You want love, you're gonna have to call the other side."

I give him a withering look. "Just give me what you use to infect. I'll twist it."

With a puzzled look, he hands me a small tablet.

I hold it up between my thumb and forefinger and frown at it. "You use this?" I scoff.

"Hey, it works," he says, insulted.

I shrug. "Not judging...not," I say as Drescal snickers in the corner.

I pinch it, crushing it and drop it into the bowl, muttering the words from the codex as I first read them; meht evol.

There is a loud bang and a fizzle as red smoke drifts up, making me cough. "Now drink it," I splutter to my circle.

Salax steps forward, hands outstretched.

"Not you, you prick," Devlin says and shoves him out of the way, reaching for the bowl himself.

I watch as everyone except Salax and Shax drink from the bowl. I keep a close eye on Gregory, but he seems to be just fine.

"Annabelle," Sid says to me quietly, but says nothing else.

"Everything okay?" I ask, taking his hand.

"I just...do you need me?" he asks, looking more unsettled than usual.

"Yes, I do, Sid. I know that asking you to be a part of this is troubling for you, but I *do* need you."

He nods and squeezes my hand. "I wasn't asking because of me," he says. "I just wondered if I hold the same weight as the others here," he adds quietly.

"Oh, Sid," I say and take him in my arms. "When will you accept that I love you? It doesn't matter to me that we haven't expressed that with our bodies yet. We will. I will wait for you to be ready. That doesn't take *anything* away from how I feel about you. If anything, it only makes me feel more."

He tightens his hold on me. "I love you," he murmurs in my ear. "Thank you for loving me."

"You make it easy," I whisper and pull back a bit so that I can kiss him. I swish my tongue against his as the room goes silent.

"How come he gets to seal it with a kiss?" Devlin asks.

I giggle as I pull back from the kiss, relieved that they accept this will happen at some point.

"I need it more than you," Sid says with a little laugh, to my surprise.

He seems to be regaining some confidence and I'm glad that he feels more comfortable in my circle.

"Well," Devlin huffs. "I'm feeling in need of a bit of reassurance myself, Annie." He saunters over to me and Sid steps back to let Devlin swoop in and then it turns into a free for all. All of my males line up to seal the deal and then I look at Xavi, standing a bit further away.

She gives me a shy smile and when I crook my finger at her, she sidles over and presses her lips to mine. "I'm still unsure of my place here," she whispers against my lips.

"Don't be," I whisper back, brushing her hair off her face. "You belong here."

She beams at me and steps back.

"Okay, so let's do this," I say. "Salax, thank you for your contribution."

Drescal gives him a rough shove, "That means you can fuck off now," he says.

Salax's eyes bore into mine and I feel myself get a bit sweaty.

He bows and says, "Always at your service, my Queen." Then, he disappears.

"*He* is trouble," Drescal says, pointing where Salax was just standing.

"Leave it now," Aleister says mildly. "Killian is right, we need to get a move on."

I press my lips together and nod. "Everyone ready?"

I get affirmations in return, even from Gregory, with no hesitation at all.

"Wait!" he says suddenly, putting his hand up. "What exactly am I supposed to do?"

"Just stand there," Elijah says. He is looking a lot better

since he took a big swig of my blood, to my relief. I was starting to worry about him. You know, maybe.

"Not helpful," Gregory spits out.

"No, he's right," I placate him. "Killian and I will do all of the heavy lifting. All you need to do is stand there. You'll feel a small pull on your essence, err, *soul*," I amend with an apologetic look, "but that's all. Is that okay?" I ask, needing him to confirm this. If he has any doubts, this isn't going to work.

He nods grimly.

"Okay, then," I say and wave my hand in a wide circle to encompass everyone in the room. We arrive back in the cavern, deep under Hell. I feel the sweat on my skin and take in a deep, heady breath to fill my lungs with the blistering air.

Lucifer is still in his Devil form, as expected, and beating and kicking the forcefield with everything that he has.

I cast a glance at Gregory to see how he is holding up.

He is drenched in sweat, unsurprisingly. The air remains a nice temperature in the residence and that is the only place he has been since he got here. Even *I* find it too hot down here. Elijah, on the other hand, seems perfectly at home.

"Everyone okay?" I ask.

Gregory, Aleister, Devlin and Drescal are all staring up at Lucifer, not so much in terror but in awe. It really pisses me off. I want them to look at *me* that way, not him.

"All good," comes the muttered reply.

"Sure?" I press.

"Yes," Gregory replies for everyone else.

I look at Sid and he looks completely disinterested in Lucifer. His eyes are only on me. I fall even more in love with him and give him a soft smile.

"Shift?" Elijah asks, pulling my focus away from Sid.

"Not necessary, unless that is your preference. Although, if you do, please don't eat anyone."

He snorts with mirth. "I'll try not to."

He Shifts as I prepare myself for the spell by closing my eyes. I breathe in deeply again.

"I will have to Shift now," I tell them, so they know it's coming. "Form a semi-circle around the mouth of the cavern. Leave the top spot for me."

I hear the scrape of boots across the ground, along with the loud tap of Elijah's claws. I also hear something that makes me crack an eye open. I gasp at the sheer beauty of the two beasts that take the spaces on either side of the cavern. War and Pestilence have Shifted to their Hellforms and they are magnificent.

They all are.

Aleister is in his Gargoyle form, Sid as his Night Mare, Devlin has pulled the cloak of death around him and Drescal has orange flames of desire licking up from his skin.

"I feel pretty useless," Gregory says loudly, but not in a way that makes me think he is bitter about it.

I snort, but the Shift has started to descend so I don't answer him. He knows that I need him.

"Oh, isn't this sweet," Lucifer growls at us, raking his talons down the forcefield.

I open both of my eyes to see it bounce and shimmer. It will break in minutes. We are cutting this way too fine.

"You still won't be able to beat me, *girl*," he snarls. "I've used my power for thousands of years. I know it."

"As I know mine," I grate out, now fully Devil'ed out and standing nearly as tall as him with my goat's head and hooves, a spiky tail, elongated horns, rows of sharp teeth and razor-like talons.

"Unholy shit," I hear Gregory murmur and now I know that all eyes are on me. The way it should be.

229

"You going to remain standing?" Devlin asks him.

"Uh-huh," he replies, gazing up at me with something that goes way past awe. Reverence is probably what it is.

I hold my hands out, palms facing each other. I start to grow a ball of Hellfire between them, starting off small but getting larger and larger.

"Ready?" I ask, and without waiting for an answer, I let Killian push as much power into me as he can.

CHAPTER 39

Annabelle

THE POWER of my circle is reverberating around my body, making me want to stumble, but I won't. I can't. Simple as that. I draw my hands out further and further as the ball grows bigger.

"You can do this, Annabelle," Gregory murmurs. I can hear him over the firestorm that is rising on either side of the forcefield. Lucifer isn't taking this sitting down and he is about to blast his way through the barrier and kill all of us, or at the very least, wish we had never been born. If I don't get this ball twice its size in the seconds I have until Lucifer is ready, then I'll have failed.

I don't take my eyes off him. I just concentrate more and feel the power washing over me. I can feel the love and respect coming from my circle. Heavy doses of lust peek through as well, which makes me smile in my head. There's something else as well, but I can't put my finger on it. It is almost like a contented happiness from deep within.

Shax, who had remained out of the way while the circle

gathered, steps up next to me now. "Drop the barrier, Sis. We're ready."

I don't answer him, I just give him a brief nod. My Hellfire ball is now bigger than the one I made Lucifer stumble with. I can do this.

I can.

I have to.

If I don't, then he will start with Gregory and eat every single one of the beings I care about.

Love. Love is the answer to beating Lucifer

Just say it, bitch. Love, love, love.

"Love!" I shout, ripping my throat apart and pull my hands back as the ball is so big now it is burning my hands.

"Step back," Shax says to the circle, knowing that I can't.

As they fall back, Lucifer breaks the barrier and with a terrifying roar, he lunges forward.

Shax throws the dagger with an accuracy that I could kiss him for, and it buries itself in Lucifer's chest, making him howl and as I'd hoped, he loses his Shift.

"Fuck you! You little shit!" he thunders, slapping his hand over the hilt, but it burns him. It is Shax's blade. Only he and I can touch it. It is doing the job I needed it to do. It is weakening Lucifer.

In the next second, I push my hands out and send the ball of fire flying across the cavern to hit him full on.

He screams, squirming from the burn, but it isn't enough.

"Again," Killian says to me now in human form, gripping my elbow tightly. "You can do this, Anna."

I draw in a deep breath. A lot quicker than the first one, another ball grows between my hands, then two. Killian is giving me everything that he has and so is everyone else. They are behind me, surrounding me, not abandoning me.

I step forward and Killian lets me go. The fire is glowing

brightly, almost screaming at me to throw them, to use them to annihilate.

I don't disappoint.

I shove out both of my hands and the two fireballs fly forward, slamming into Lucifer at the same time and bursting into the fires of Hell that burns him to an ash as we watch.

Silence.

I blink.

"Is that it?" Devlin asks.

I turn my Devil's head to glare at him. He feels my wrath and actually quakes in his boots. "Is that it?" I snarl at him.

I am fucked. Well and truly fucked. How I'm still standing on my shaky hooves is a mystery.

I put my hand to my head and allow the Shift to retreat, stumbling but Killian is there to catch me.

"You did it," he says with a smile.

"*We* did it," I reply and then slump into his embrace.

"Not to be the party pooper and incur your wrath," Gregory ventures. "But is it over?"

"I'm glad that *you* said that and not me," Aleister mutters.

"Yes, it's over," I say. "Love was the key."

I climb out of Killian's arms. I walk over to the pile of ash that used to be Lucifer and glare down at it. I hold my hand out and sweep the ashes into a small, neat pile and then summon up a black velvet drawstring bag. I transfer the contents of the ash to the bag and then, with the flick of my wrist, send them into their own little firecube on the other side of Hell from Leviathan.

Just in case.

CHAPTER 40

I TURN BACK to my circle with a tired but bright smile.

"Thanks," I mutter, shoving my sweaty, messy hair back.

"What for?" Elijah asks. "We didn't do anything really."

"You didn't leave me," I say and feel the stupid tears prick my eyes.

"No fucking chance of that," Drescal says. "You are stuck with us, I'm afraid."

I giggle. "I can't think of a better group to be stuck with."

"Aww," Devlin says, looking away and sniffing.

"You ass," I say, shaking my head at him.

He turns back and grins. "So, anyone else *really* horny now?"

I raise my hand with a cheeky grin.

"Oh, for fuck's sake," Shax mutters and disappears. I don't care that he didn't congratulate me or any of that other bullshit. I know how he feels.

"I guess it's just us then," I say and whisk us all back to my bedroom.

Sid catches my eye and gives me a smile before he slips

out of the room. I let him go because now isn't the time for us to be together.

I do look over at Gregory and although he is covered in sweat and filth, he doesn't appear to be going anywhere. I give him a smirk. "Want to take a shower?"

He lets out a guffaw, that some of the others look confused at, and says, "Thought you'd never ask."

I hold my hand out and lead him into the bathroom, telling the others we won't be long. I snap my fingers and lose the clothes that reappeared after my Shift.

His eyes heat up and he lets me undress him slowly, seductively as Xavi joins us.

Gregory looks at her, but then ignores her as she slips her ice-blue dress off and turns on the shower. She steps in and makes way for me to pull Gregory inside.

Xavi hands me the soap and I start to lather it in between my hands. I give it back to her and then soap up Gregory, lingering on his stiff cock more than I should have. He groans and throws his head back.

I can't help but fall to my knees and take him in my mouth.

He grunts and shoves his hand into my hair. I graze my teeth down his length gently and then back up to swirl my tongue over his tip.

"Annabelle," he cries out and gushes his cum into my mouth in a hot, deliciousness that makes me moan and swallow it all.

Xavi pulls me up and proceeds to wash me down as Gregory pants and recovers from my attention to his cock.

Xavi takes the soap and rubs it between my tits and then over my peaked nipples. Gregory's eyes are riveted to the scene. He is panting now for a whole other reason.

She slides it down my body and over my branded pussy before she replaces it on the dish and moves me under the water to rinse me off, taking one of my nipples in her mouth to suck into an even harder peak.

"Touch her," she murmurs to Gregory.

He is hesitant at first, but as soon as he places his hand on my pussy, he gains his confidence. He flicks my clit and I cry out softly, getting wetter as he slides his fingers inside me.

"Yes," I murmur, running my hand into his hair and pushing him down.

He smiles and moves into position to take his tongue and run it down my slit and back up to my swollen clit. He sucks it into his mouth, and I come with a gasp, clenching around his fingers still buried inside me.

"Mm," he murmurs and grinds his teeth down on me gently.

"Fuck," I pant. "More."

He stands up and Xavi lets me go so that he can sweep me up into his arms and carry me back to the bedroom. He places me on the bed, where the other males are waiting for me, naked and very ready. I kneel in the middle of the bed and pull Drescal to me. I kiss him deeply, swishing my tongue over his, wrapping my arms around him. Devlin lifts my leg up, holding it in place as Drescal swiftly enters me, shoving his cock deep. Devlin moves my leg to rest on Drescal's shoulder as my Incubus gives me a good fuck that makes me come quickly and easily, especially after Gregory and Xavi warmed me up.

"No words," I murmur to them as Drescal places me on top of Aleister. I wiggle around, squashing my tits against his chest as he guides his dick into my pussy. Drescal lubes up my rear hole and shoves his way inside with Devlin next to him.

I cry out at the massive invasion, loving every second of this. I rear up slightly so that Xavi can return to sucking my nipple, her hand dropping lower to circle my clit as Aleister rams up into me, his fingers digging into my hips painfully hard. The orgasm that builds up starts at my toes, burning its way through my veins until I explode around Aleister's dick, clutching him so tightly he grunts as he spurts his load.

Xavi slips her fingers into my pussy, before Aleister can pull out, which fires up my burning lust again.

She kisses me, tugging on my nipple with one hand while the other one finger fucks me. Aleister starts to move again.

"Fuck, fuck," Devlin pants and then groans as he fills my ass with cum, followed shortly by Drescal.

They both pull out at the same time and I give them a creampie. The animalistic noise that follows, comes from Gregory. He reaches out to wipe the cum away and then slips his finger in my ass.

"I've never…" he says shyly.

"Oh, you must," Devlin encourages him and moves aside.

I look over my shoulder to see that Gregory is more than ready to penetrate me. I give him a wicked smile and look into Xavi's eyes as he positions himself gently and eases himself in.

"Fuck, that's tight," he mutters.

"Mm," Drescal murmurs.

"Oh, yes." Gregory withdraws and then pumps his hips, fucking my ass as he makes a satisfied noise that makes me giggle.

We go back to saying nothing as Gregory drills my ass harder and harder until, panting like a dog, he stiffens and unloads into me.

"One more to go and you've had all of me," I say seductively, making Elijah pounce on me, whisking me away from the other males and Xavi, to land on the floor on my back with him on top of me.

"My turn," he growls and grinds his hips against mine as he skewers me on his dick.

He pounds me into the carpet as I wrap my legs around him.

"Fuck, yes, puppy," I rasp, the climax building up and tumbling over, making me shudder underneath him.

I catch Killian's eyes. He is calmly watching this from the armchair, naked and glorious.

"I'll have my turn in a bit, Princess," he says quietly. "Enjoy the others, for when I take you, it will be just the two of us."

I purr in response and flip Elijah over so that I can ride him and let the others sweep down to lick, bite, suck, kiss, flick, pinch and scrape every inch of my skin until Elijah bursts his banks and floods my pussy. I grip him tightly with my walls until he gasps for mercy.

"Fuck, Anna," he pants. "Fuck."

Killian stands up then and drags me off Elijah's still stiff cock, turning me in his arms. I wrap my legs around him, wanting him to take me where we stand.

He does.

Elijah guides Killian's massive length into my dripping cunt as we stare into each other's eyes. I start to ride him slowly at first, but then in a frenzy, needing to feel every inch of him rubbing over my g-spot.

"Yes, yes, yes!" I scream as my orgasm thunders over me. "Tell me I'm your dirty whore, War. Call me filthy and a slut!"

"No, my love," he says quietly. "You are my everything."

"Fuck you!" I roar as my cunt responds to his words against my wishes. I don't want it giving him what he wants. Asshole.

But I drench him anyway, coating his cock with my cream and he gives me a perfectly innocent smile that makes me shake my head at him.

"You're a dick," I pant.

He grabs my hips tighter and pumps me up and down,

taking control and using me to pleasure him.

"You're a cunt," he says with a smirk.

"Fuck you!"

"Already am."

"Rah!" I shout in his face and come again, pulsing around him fiercely and throwing my head back.

Elijah catches me and lays me out. Drescal and Devlin grab my legs and pull them away from Killian to open wide.

War fucks me as I'm held in place in midair, pounding away until I've lost count of the number of times I've come. I'm practically limp by the time he grunts and dumps his cum in my cunt.

I'm placed back on the bed, but he isn't finished with me yet.

"Please your female, slut. I want to watch you suck her clit and tongue fuck her until she screams your name."

Xavi gasps as she has suddenly become the center of attention. She shakes her head at me, but I beckon her over.

"I want to taste you," I say. "I want my hot tongue up your icy cunt."

"Fuck," she breathes and loses herself to me.

She lies back and I part her legs as the males watch us, dicks in their hands. They surround the bed, jerking themselves off as I slowly run my tongue over her pussy and then into her. She hisses at the sizzle and then squirms to get closer to my mouth.

"Oh, Belle," she says and gives into it.

I take her clit in between my teeth and tug gently until she writhes on the black silk sheets. I thrust two fingers into her, finger fucking her until she cries out. I suck her clit into my mouth and then flick the hard nub with the tip of my tongue.

"Fuck," she pants as she bucks on the bed.

The males are getting more worked up as they watch this.

They pump away at their dicks, closing in on us by kneeling on the bed now.

"Come for me," I murmur to her. "I want to taste that sweet cum."

I thrust my tongue inside her, putting pressure on her clit with my thumb.

She screams my name as the wave of ecstasy crashes over her and she shudders on the bed.

Splats of male cum land on us as they can't contain their lust at seeing me fuck another female with my mouth.

"Belle!" Xavi cries out and convulses again as I don't give up my relentless tongue-fuck.

I pull away with a soft smile at Killian. "Does that please you?" I ask.

"It does," he says and then drags me to him to start the ravaging of my cunt with his dick all over again, this time allowing my other males to take turns with my ass.

Later that night, I lie in bed, surrounded by my circle. I wish that Sid was here, but our time will come. I have faith in us.

I place my hand on my stomach and feel a small buzz of power under my palm. It's like an electric shock and makes me draw my hand back with a frown.

I climb carefully off the bed so that I don't disturb anyone and pull on a robe, looking out over the sin bin.

That contented happiness that I felt during the spell pops back up and I try to push it away. I try to ignore it, but it doesn't want to be ignored. It wants to be acknowledged.

"Go away," I hiss. "I don't want you."

"Belle?" Xavi asks, yawning and climbing off the bed to join. "Is everything okay? You look pale." She reaches out to stroke my face.

"No," I whisper. "Everything has gone to Hell."

"Lucifer?" she asks and looks out over the sin bin.

I shake my head. "I can't do this."

She takes my hand. "Do what?" she asks quietly.

"Be a mother," I whisper so quietly, I don't think she heard me at first.

"What?" she asks, raising her eyebrow.

"I think I'm pregnant," I murmur. "I can *feel* the presence inside me."

"Oh," she says. "Uhm, do you know which one?" She frowns at me and shakes her head. "Probably not."

"I have no idea. I didn't think it was possible without a Demon Bound, or the male version of it," I answer starting to panic.

"Are you sure?" she asks. "About the child."

"I think so," I say, gripping her hands. "I can't do this, Xavier. I don't want to be a mother. I don't…I can't…it's not me."

"It's okay," she says. "You don't have to do anything yet."

I nod. "Yes, okay," I say, but then my face crumples. "I need to get out of here," I say desperately.

"Come," she says. "I know somewhere we can go."

"Anna?" Elijah asks, sitting up on the bed and disturbing the other males. "What's going on?"

"I can't do this! I have to go!" I blurt out and give a nod to Xavi, who is ready to whisk us away. The last thing I see is the males leap off the bed, hands trying to get to me, concern in their voices as they ask what I mean.

"I'm sorry," I say and let Xavi take me away, hoping that what I feel inside me is wrong.

The End

ABOUT THE AUTHOR

Eve is a British novelist with a specialty for paranormal romance, with strong female leads, causing her to develop a Reverse Harem Fantasy series, several years ago: The Forever Series.

She lives in the UK, with her husband and four kids, so finding the time to write is short, but definitely sweet. She currently has two on-going series, with a number of spin-offs in the making. Eve hopes to release some new and exciting projects in the next couple of years, so stay tuned!

Start Eve's Reverse Harem Fantasy Series, with the first two books in the Forever Series as a double edition!

Newsletter Sign up for exclusive content and giveaways: **http://eepurl.com/bxilBT**

Facebook Reader Group: https://www.facebook.com/groups/ForeverEves

Facebook: http://facebook.com/evenewtonforever

Twitter: https://twitter.com/AuthorEve

Website: https://evenewtonauthor.com/

ALSO BY EVE NEWTON

Dark Fae's Desires

Dark Fae's Secrets

Enchained Hearts Series:

Lives Entwined

Lives Entangled

Lives Endangered

The Bound Series:

Demon Bound

Demon Freed

Demon Returned

Demon Queen Series:

Hell's Belle

Pandora's Box

Circle of Darkness:

Wild Hearts: Book One

Savage Love: Book Two

Tainted Blood: Book Three

Dark Hearts - A Prequel

Darkest Desires: Book Four

The Early Years Series:

Aefre & Constantine 1 & 2

Printed in Poland
by Amazon Fulfillment
Poland Sp. z o.o., Wrocław

61875154R00148